COLTON FAMILY BODYGUARD

Jennifer Morey

HARLEQUIN

ROMANTIC
SUSPENSE

Special thanks and acknowledgment are given to
Jennifer Morey for her contribution to
The Coltons of Mustang Valley miniseries.

HARLEQUIN®
ROMANTIC SUSPENSE™

Recycling programs
for this product may
not exist in your area.

ISBN-13: 978-1-335-62640-0

Colton Family Bodyguard

Copyright © 2020 by Harlequin Books S.A.

This edition published by arrangement with Harlequin Books S.A.

For questions and comments about the quality of this book, please contact us at CustomerService@Harlequin.com.

Harlequin Enterprises ULC
22 Adelaide St. West, 40th Floor
Toronto, Ontario M5H 4E3, Canada
www.Harlequin.com

Printed in U.S.A.

In her silence, Callum stepped closer to her. He put his fingers beneath her chin. Heat coursed through her as she tried to figure out why he had touched her this way.

"It's more than wanting you safe, Hazel. I have a personal reason for doing so. You see, I normally don't take cases involving women and children. Protecting them. It just so happens that I fell into protecting you and Evie and now I cannot turn my back. I have to see this through."

He seemed to be trying to make her understand why it was so important to him that she stay here in their suite. She still didn't get it. He had to see this through...but why *him*? Why didn't he take cases involving women and children? Why make such a pledge?

"I can't explain it right now. All I ask is you trust me," he said.

After a moment of stunned perplexity, she nodded. She wouldn't press him now, but the need to know would gnaw at her until he told her everything. If he ever did...

* * *

Book 3 of The Coltons of Mustang Valley

* * *

If you're on Twitter, tell us what you think of Harlequin Romantic Suspense! #harlequinromsuspense

Dear Reader,

Welcome to another fun-filled Colton series book! I don't have the opportunity to do bodyguard books very often, especially one where a child witnesses a murder. This one was special for me. The plot fell right into place with characters who really moved the story for me. Little Evie is as adorable as can be!

One of the elements I liked most—and hope you find enjoyable as well—was the heroine's and hero's past heartbreaks and how that played into their reluctance to get involved. Writing their emotional growth felt honest and rewarding. And of course, who doesn't love a good Colton book?

Sincerely yours,

Jennifer

Two-time RITA® Award nominee and Golden Quill award winner **Jennifer Morey** writes single-title contemporary romance and page-turning romantic suspense. She has a geology degree and has managed export programs in compliance with the International Traffic in Arms Regulations (ITAR) for the aerospace industry. She lives at the foot of the Rocky Mountains in Denver, Colorado, and loves to hear from readers through her website, jennifermorey.com, or Facebook.

Books by Jennifer Morey

Harlequin Romantic Suspense

The Coltons of Mustang Valley

Colton Family Bodyguard

Cold Case Detectives

A Wanted Man
Justice Hunter
Cold Case Recruit
Taming Deputy Harlow
Runaway Heiress
Hometown Detective
Cold Case Manhunt

The Coltons of Roaring Springs

Colton's Convenient Bride

The Coltons of Red Ridge

Colton's Fugitive Family

Visit Jennifer's Author Profile page at
Harlequin.com, or jennifermorey.com,
for more titles.

For my family, for always supporting me and the time I spend writing.

Chapter 1

Why did every woman he met and thought might be the one always announce at the worst possible time that she wanted babies? Callum Colton walked along a street at the edge of Mustang Valley, Arizona, on a sunny, early spring day. He had just left his now ex-girlfriend, Cindy, in tears because he'd had to tell her he was never going to have any children. He'd explained that to her at the beginning but she must have thought she could change his mind. He'd had to remind her he meant what he'd said. In truth, he felt so rotten, ending the relationship like that. She'd told him she understood and held no animosity toward him, but she was obviously very hurt.

Callum stepped into Executive Protection Services, LLC still lamenting what had happened. What else could he have done? He would have hurt his ex-girlfriend more had he continued on with her. When Cindy sat him down for The Serious Talk, she'd told him she wanted children and she wanted them with him. She loved him, and her biological clock ticked on and she felt she had to move now. That convinced him they weren't right for each other. She had hoped he felt the same as her and that he would give her children. She hadn't anticipated how unbending he was on the matter. And the truth was that he did not love her. They would have ended their relationship eventually, since she wanted a family. Why drag it out? He never had serious relationships with women he dated. How had she gotten the impression he would with her? He had told her as much. He almost shuddered as the door closed behind him and he walked through the entry with its vacant reception desk toward an office in the back.

He had enough going on without having to now feel guilty for hurting Cindy. He was still reeling from the news that his half brother, Ace, had been switched at birth and wasn't really his biological sibling. Not by blood. Who would do such a thing and why? The why of it really twisted his mind. Charles, the owner, chief executive officer, president and whatever other titles a guy like him liked to have, looked up from behind his metal-and-glass desk. The lack of clutter and nearly bare walls pretty much described him. Focused. Nothing personal. Good business head. That's why Callum had agreed to work for him. Callum had no liking for paper-work. Charles did.

"It's about time you got here." Charles stood and moved around his desk.

"I had to take care of something." Cindy's tear-damp cheeks flashed through his mind. Chaos had reigned recently in his life, ever since an email had made the rounds of his family's company, Colton Oil, saying that his oldest brother, Ace, was not a biological Colton. Since then, his father, Payne, had been shot—and now the cops even suspected Ace.

Charles stopped before him and cocked his head. "Well, that sounds like you. When you need to take care of something, nothing keeps you from doing it—not even your boss."

"I broke up with my girlfriend," Callum said.

"Another one? The hot blonde? What's wrong with you?"

Callum put his hands up. "She wanted kids."

Charles's brow creased a little. "What is it with you and kids? They're harmless and adorable. Who wouldn't want them?"

"Not me."

"Why not? They can be challenging sometimes but the rewards far outweigh that."

Charles had two young kids. He had a wife and a nice house. A real family man. "Why did you call me here?" Callum asked in irritation.

After considering him awhile, Charles said, "You never talk about anything, do you realize that?"

Callum angled his head in silent warning.

"Keeping things bottled up is unhealthy. I worry about you."

Callum said nothing and continued to look at him.

"Why do you think I called you here?" Charles asked.

Callum had a pretty good idea why. And he also thought this was going to be a waste of time. "I got the job done and the client is alive." He'd done a job as a bodyguard for an executive who had a stalker.

"I'm not telling you to change your ways." Charles scoffed. "I couldn't anyway. But for the welfare of this company, I am telling you to be more careful. I almost couldn't convince the police you didn't break the law."

The stalker had gotten too close to his delicate female client and Callum had given him a clear… message. Someone must have called 911 because the police had arrived after Callum and his client left.

"You were lucky the stalker was wanted for sexual assault on another woman. If they hadn't been able to arrest him, they probably wouldn't have let you go with just a warning," his boss said.

Callum walked over to the window and passively watched cars go by and a man walking his dog on the sidewalk.

"Seriously, Callum, you can't make up your own rules as you go."

Why was Charles rambling on so long about that? Hopefully Callum had knocked some sense into him. Charles was just uncomfortable about employing a man who wasn't afraid to cross boundaries.

"I'll be careful, Charles," Callum said.

"Why does that sound so half-baked?"

Callum glanced back with a rueful grin. "Because it is. Stop worrying so much. You're not the one who would have been arrested, and protecting our clients won't damage our reputation. If anything, it will get us more business."

"You can't protect anyone if you're in jail."

Turning back to the window, Callum said, "I didn't cross the line. We advertise elite services, don't we?" The view distracted him a moment. Charles had rented an office in an attractive one-story mall with a restaurant and a gas station beside the parking lot. The back of the building faced a quiet, tree-lined road. Across the street an upscale subdivision sprawled.

"Okay, but just don't get caught."

"I knew that stalker was wanted for assault. I found out two days ago."

"You still could have been arrested, Callum. Even criminals have rights."

"I'll keep that in mind." Or not. Callum's first priority was protecting his clients. He had a strong conviction about that. Victims didn't deserve to be forced into being victims. The menace that threatened them was a cancer that had to be carved out and stopped. That's what had led him to a career as a bodyguard, and back home to support his family in a time of crisis.

"It turns out that's not the only reason I asked you

to stop by. I've got another case for you. Ever hear of the country singer Blake Reynolds?"

"No." Callum liked country but didn't pay attention to the artists' names.

Outside, a black Mercedes SUV—one of the more economical versions—pulled to a stop on the side of the street. Callum caught sight of a woman with long dark hair in the driver's seat. She had a fantastic profile. At the same time, a car stopped on the side of the street about two houses down.

Callum listened to Charles explain the new case while he turned back to the woman, who climbed out of the SUV and opened the back door. She worked to free a little girl from a car seat. Normally this was when he would have turned away from the sight of a mother and her child, but something about the woman made him keep watching—and stop listening to Charles. Maybe it was that tight body in those dressy black pants, or the curve of that slender waist, or the way her those perfectly shaped breasts strained against the white blouse.

She lifted the girl from the seat and lowered her to the ground. Holding a stuffed Cookie Monster in one arm, the child looked up at her mother and said something, to which the woman shook her head. The little girl didn't appear to like the answer, an adorable pout forming beneath scrunching eyebrows, and she hugged the stuffed toy against the white top of a cute flaring black skirt. He felt an automatic pang at the adorable mother-daughter duo.

The mother went to the back of the Mercedes and

lifted the hatch. Callum got a really nice view of her frame as she leaned in and retrieved two recyclable grocery bags. Setting those on the pavement, she reached in again and handed a plastic container to the little girl, who still frowned and continued to argue with her mother.

The beautiful woman crouched before her, her facial features striking him to the core. She spoke to the girl, whose frown finally smoothed.

Standing, the woman closed the hatch and lifted the bags, talking with the young girl. The child walked with short, clumsy steps beside her mother up the driveway to the front door of a house. When they disappeared inside, Callum realized how immersed he'd become in watching the woman and child. His stomach fell.

Then he looked down the street and saw the car that had pulled over was still there, with someone sitting in the driver's seat. A man. He appeared to be watching the woman's house, though he was too far away to get a good look inside. Out of habit, Callum checked the license plate but it was too far away to make out.

Charles appeared beside him, looking from the house across the street to him. "Have you heard a single word I've said?"

"Sorry, no." Callum turned away from the window.

"The singer had a girlfriend who's gone off the deep end. He's afraid she'll go after him."

"Another one of those cases?" Only this time it would be a man he protected.

"They were together for six months and she started to get too clingy, so he ended it. He said he noticed other things, too, like catching her in lies. She told her friends they were getting married. She also told him she was pregnant but she wasn't. He made her do a test and it was negative. When he asked why she lied, she said she was afraid she was going to lose him."

"Does he have any kids?" Callum asked.

"No. You've made it perfectly clear you don't want those kinds of cases—which you still haven't told me why." Charles looked out the window again. "I meant what I said about keeping things bottled up, Callum."

"When do I go?" He didn't like talking about why he never took mother-child cases. Charles tried to get him to every once in a while and Callum believed that Charles was concerned about him. He had become a good friend, aside from being Callum's boss.

"He's local. That's how he heard of you."

"Me?"

"Yeah. He asked for you by name. You'll be working with his usual security team."

"He doesn't think his own team will be enough?" What kind of woman had this new client broken up with?

Charles walked back to his desk and picked up a folder. "I printed these out for you. I also emailed them. You'll understand more after you read it. He's out of the country right now, but asked if you could stay at his place next month."

Callum took the file. "Thanks." Charles knew he liked studying cases on paper more than on a screen. Some things were still better offline, like holding a book instead of a tablet.

"Any news on your father?" Charles asked.

"He's still in a coma. I'm heading over to the hospital after I go see my brother." Payne Colton had been shot after receiving a bizarre email containing the shocking news about Ace. He didn't say which brother he was going to see, since Ace was still a suspect in Payne's shooting. When Callum and his twin sister—current Colton Oil CEO Marlowe—had visited Mustang Valley General Hospital last month, they were told that a fire broke out the morning of Ace's birth and destroyed all records.

With one more look out the window that told him the car and the man were still there, Callum bade Charles farewell and left the building. But he couldn't stop thinking about that parent and child. He couldn't explain why he needed to make sure she was all right. A sixth sense told him something was off about the stranger in the car. Even though he had sworn off guarding families, he couldn't ignore this. He'd make sure the woman and her daughter were okay and then he'd be on his way.

Hazel Hart took her now-cheerful daughter's hand and walked with her toward the SUV. Earlier Evie had fussed about being told she could not go for ice cream today. Hazel's schedule was far too busy. But Evie liked passing out cookies to Hazel's clients.

Hazel had told her five-year-old she could sample one with them. That had taken care of the ice cream tantrum.

Hazel glanced around. The street was quiet. This area of town didn't get much traffic. On the edge of Mustang Valley, there was a lot of new development and not much commercial business. The back of the strip mall across the street hid most of the activity there, though landscaping along the sidewalk made it more palatable for residents. The client she'd just left enjoyed the convenience of Hazel's home deliveries, especially since she had been taken ill with breast cancer. The woman was going to be all right, but had hired Hazel to provide her meals while she recovered. The woman had family but they all lived out of state and she didn't like the food her neighbors prepared.

Hazel had left her job at an upscale restaurant several months ago to go off on her own as a personal chef. She preferred the independence and not having to work under someone else's thumb. Plus, she could always be with Evie, which was her most favorite thing in the world.

Reaching the SUV, Hazel unlocked it and had her hand on the back seat door handle when Evie said, "Mommy, what is that man doing?"

Hazel looked in the direction Evie pointed and saw a man in a blue sedan, wearing sunglasses and a baseball cap.

"Why did he hit that man over the head with a rock and put him in the car?"

Hazel turned sharply to Evie. "What?" She looked around and didn't see anything.

Evie pointed. "That man put another man in the trunk, Mommy."

Hazel felt a wave of apprehension sweep through her as she stared at the sedan. If the driver had struck a man unconscious and put him into the trunk, he could not have any good intentions. He started pulling out into the street way too quickly for Hazel's comfort.

Hazel memorized the license plate as the man began driving along the street, right toward them.

Reaching for Evie's hand, she went to pull her daughter onto the sidewalk. Evie dropped her Cookie Monster and bent to pick it up. Horror flared up in Hazel. She glanced up and saw the car was almost on them! They'd be run over!

"Evie—" Just then someone swooped Evie up and grabbed Hazel's hand, yanking her backward.

The stranger in the sedan continued to race for them. Hazel screamed, as did Evie, as a man hauled them behind her Mercedes and up onto the sidewalk. The other car whizzed past, taking out her Mercedes' driver-side mirror.

"Are you all right?"

Hazel pulled her hand from the man's, heart flying and struggling to catch her breath. A car had just tried to mow them down! The sound of the Mercedes mirror being torn off kept echoing in her mind.

She reached for a crying Evie. The heroic man handed her daughter over and Hazel held her tightly.

"It's okay, baby. We're all right." She looked at the man as she answered his question.

Hazel checked up the street and saw no sign of the driver. Then she turned back to her hero. "Thank you."

He took out his phone and called 911.

Her adrenaline began to abate as Evie's crying softened. Smoothing the few tendrils of brunette hair that had fallen free from the two ponytails sticking out from the sides of Evie's head, she wiped her daughter's cheeks.

Looking over the child's shoulder, she saw the man as more than her rescuer. His reddish-blond hair was slightly wavy and he had strong facial features. He wore dark slacks with black leather loafers that had thick soles, and between the lapels of his black jacket she could see he had on a white shirt with the first two buttons undone. He finished telling the operator where they were and disconnected. Towering above her, he was probably six-three and had an athletic build.

"I'm Callum Colton," the handsome man said.

"Hazel Hart, and this is Evie, short for Evelyn."

Evie turned her head, still pouting, and looked at Callum.

"Hi, Evie. Are you okay?" Callum asked.

Evie nodded.

"That's an awfully cute stuffed monster you have there," he said.

"Her name is Cookie," Evie said, brightening.

He chuckled and glanced at Hazel, who became transfixed by his smile. "That's appropriate."

Well, whether he was a kid person or not, his tactics worked. Ever since Ed ran out on her after hearing she was pregnant, Hazel always wondered whether or not a man who caught her eyes liked children.

"I think Evie saw something," Hazel said. "She said a man hit another one over the head with a rock and put him into the trunk."

The faint sound of sirens joined the gentle hum of distant town movements. Hazel put Evie down and held her hand, needing to have contact with her. Having nearly been run down by a car had rattled them both. To think Evie could have been hurt, or worse...

"Did you see him, too?" Callum asked.

She shook her head. "He was in the car already when I saw him. I didn't get a good look at him. I did get the plate number, though."

"That's great." Then he asked Evie, "Can you describe the man?"

The little girl nodded. "Mm-hmm. He looked really mad."

"Mad?" Hazel asked, prompting her to elaborate.

Evie crowded her tiny eyebrows over eyes that were greener than her mother's. "Yeah." Evie nodded. "He looked like the man at the mall, Mommy."

Hazel met her daughter's round, innocent eyes, heart melting as usual at Evie's adorableness and also searching for the memory. Then she recalled a homeless man they had encountered at the edge of the parking lot. He had been dressed in heavy clothing and had a beard, a dark beard.

"Was the man you saw as hairy as the man in the parking lot earlier?" Hazel asked.

"No, he was not skinny. And no hair on his face."

The homeless man had been slim and had a beard. "The man she saw was average in height and weight," Hazel said.

The sirens were now a blaring howl and seconds later, fire trucks, police cars and ambulances converged upon them.

"I hope this doesn't take long." Hazel had to prepare meals for tomorrow's deliveries.

"You witnessed a crime," Callum said. "The man got away. What if he comes after you again? We need to catch this guy."

Hazel hadn't considered that. Police approached and, filled with intensifying apprehension, she had to turn away from Callum's unmistakable concern. Her meals could wait. She could get up early tomorrow and prepare them.

A woman in a tan blazer approached, her strides graceful, auburn hair flowing.

"Kerry," Callum greeted her. "Good to see you again."

"Callum, what are you doing here?" Kerry's blue eyes were direct and exuded confidence.

"My office is across the street. I saw a man in a car and thought it was suspicious."

He had? Hazel looked across the street at the one-story strip mall. One of the spaces must be where Callum worked.

"This is Hazel and Evie Hart," Callum said. "This is Detective Kerry Wilder. She's also my brother Rafe's fiancée."

Hazel shook the pretty woman's hand.

"Evie here saw the man when he got out of the car," Callum said.

"You did?" Kerry asked in a lighthearted tone, crouching before the girl. "What did you see?"

Evie huddled closer to Hazel's leg, bringing Cookie up to her face. She got bashful sometimes.

"She saw the driver of the car hit another man on the head and put him in the trunk," Hazel answered for her daughter.

Kerry straightened and began writing on a small notepad.

The detective with Kerry went to take photos of Hazel's broken mirror while Hazel described the man who had almost run them down. Then she gave the detective his plate number.

"All right. We're going to talk to neighbors and tenants of the commercial building to see if there are any other witnesses," Kerry said. "Why don't you stop by the station later so we can have a sketch artist draw the man you saw?"

Hazel nodded.

"Callum, you should come, too. You can probably help with the description."

Callum nodded once.

Detective Wilder put away her notepad. "Meanwhile, we'll have officers on the lookout for this car."

And whatever he had done with the man in his trunk. Hazel warded off a shiver. If he could hurt someone like that, what would he do to Evie?

"You should be careful until we locate him. Are you or your husband armed?"

"I'm not married," Hazel said, then saw Callum glance at her at that revelation.

"Maybe you should stay somewhere else," Kerry said. Then to Callum, "I don't think they should be alone tonight."

Callum looked a little startled by the suggestion, or that Kerry had directed the declaration at him, as though he should be the one to take care of them for the night.

"Do you have any family you can stay with?" Kerry asked Hazel.

They were all far away except her brother, but he was a two hour drive from here. She shook her head.

"Friends?"

All out of state. She didn't know anyone well enough here to impose on them like that. Again, she shook her head. "All my close friends are in Colorado and I haven't had time to make any here." She looked down at Evie, who consumed every spare moment she wasn't working.

"That man could have gotten your plate number the same as you got his. He might have a way to find out where you live," the detective said. "Maybe I'm being overly paranoid, but I'd rather you be safe."

That certainly unsettled her.

Detective Wilder smiled. "I'll let you be on your way. Think about staying somewhere other than your house tonight after we finish up with the sketch, okay? Maybe get a room at the Dales Inn."

"Okay."

"What about letting Evie go to the station with Kerry for her safety? In the meantime, I'll take you home to pack bags for both of you," Callum said.

Oh. Hazel hated being separated from Evie under such dire circumstances, but her daughter seemed entranced by Kerry's shiny badge and getting her own detective shield sticker.

Hazel hesitated. "Detective Wilder is the one with the gun…"

Kerry chimed in, "Maybe Callum can help out. He's an ex-Navy SEAL turned professional bodyguard."

Evie looked at Callum. "Are you going to catch the bad man?"

Callum didn't respond, just stared at Evie as though flustered. What about her question had caused such a reaction? He seemed to be frozen.

"What if he comes after us, like you said?" Evie asked.

"I shouldn't have said that in front of you," Callum said.

"Honey, Callum isn't a policeman. He is a bodyguard," Hazel said.

"What's a bodyguard?" Evie asked.

"Someone who protects people from bad men," Callum said.

Evie smiled big and again Hazel noticed a change in Callum, the way his body stiffened. "Then you can protect me and my mommy."

He smiled down at her. "I'll try."

Evie glanced down at her toy. "It's okay, Cookie," she said. "You're all right now. Just remember, it's wrong to hit and push. You should always be nice to other people."

Hazel reached over and put her hand on Evie's. "Now you're going to the station and I will go home and pack clothing for us."

"Okay, Mommy."

It was getting late, past six in the evening. "All right," Hazel said. "Let's go."

Detective Wilder joined her partner and Evie as they walked up the street.

"Let's go to your place," Callum suggested.

The abruptness stopped Hazel short. This man was a complete stranger.

"I'd like to talk a little more," he said. "And Kerry has a point. I'm worried that man will come after you. You got his plate number. He probably got yours. He could find you."

Why was he so concerned about her? He didn't even know her. "I'm a newbie with all this. What kinds of people do you usually work with?"

"My next client is Blake Reynolds."

"The country singer? Really? You must be some bodyguard. Are all your clients celebrities?"

"Oh, all right. Let's go."

The police were still working the neighborhood but the emergency vehicles had left a while ago. Callum drove Hazel in silence to her apartment, located above a bakery. Callum had arranged for someone to take her car in for repairs. She had left a key under the mat. She might drive a Mercedes but it was the lower end model and she had saved for a long time for a decent down payment. The money she made was just enough for her and Evie to get by. So far, being a personal chef didn't earn her huge income. Her business showed signs of picking up but she wasn't quite there yet.

When they arrived at her apartment, Callum passed the front and turned to go around to the back.

The first floor of the older building was a charming little bakery with a neon Open/Closed sign on the door, four old-fashioned, small round tables in the dining area and two booths against the window. The main feature was the display case…and, of course, the kitchen. The owner of Jasmine's Bakery let her cook her biggest batches there for a modest fee.

After Callum parked, Hazel walked from the rear parking space up the iron stairs. Unlocking her apartment door, she flipped on a light and entered, Callum behind her. "It isn't much. Just two bedrooms and not very big." She didn't know why she felt the need to explain that.

Callum didn't say anything as he stepped inside, looking around.

"When my ex, Ed, walked, I started saving for a house, but I also want money tucked away for Evie's college education."

Hazel found herself looking at him, his rugged, stubbly jaw, his thick, reddish-blond hair. Her gaze moved to his bright blue eyes…and stayed. He had been watching her study his face and now his eyes flared with something more than friendliness. A spark of heat flashed inside her.

How could just a look do that to her? Did he feel it too? Granted, he was hot, but she had seen other attractive men, and none of them had caused this reaction.

"So, you're an ex-Navy SEAL and now you're a bodyguard," Hazel said by way of breaking the awkward moment. "If you're going to protect me and my daughter, I should know more than that about you."

"I'm surprised that's all you know about me," he said. "I am, after all, a Colton."

The name did sound familiar but not familiar enough. "I may have heard the name before. I haven't lived here my whole life."

"Given the news lately, you probably have. Payne Colton is my father."

Hazel searched her memory but still nothing stuck. "I'm sorry. I don't watch the news. I try to keep it away from Evie. I don't think it's healthy for a five-year-old to hear about murders and lying politicians. And besides that, I have a very busy schedule. We do watch a lot of family movies and listen to country, though." She smiled. "You might have to introduce us to Blake Reynolds."

He chuckled. "I can't believe it."

What couldn't he believe? That she didn't watch the news or that she didn't know him by name? She couldn't detect conceit. He wasn't bragging about being a Colton, just surprised she hadn't heard of them.

"My father is chairman of the board of Colton Oil and owns Rattlesnake Ridge Ranch just outside of town. But we do all work hard for our money," he said.

Then it dawned on her. She had heard of a man who had been shot and was now in a coma, a prominent local rancher and businessman gunned down for no apparent reason. She hadn't paid any further attention to the story. Until now.

"Oh, I'm so sorry," she finally said. Callum came from lots of money, then. Hazel felt herself stiffen and erect a barrier. She was from a very humble background and her last encounter with a rich guy hadn't turned out so great.

"Don't be."

"I grew up in a small Colorado mountain town where everyone knew everyone and there were no conveniences, no big-box stores, no chain restaurants or movie theaters. We lived outside of town on several acres in a small colonial. I spent my childhood reading or watching satellite television and going to community events with my older brother and our parents."

"Sounds charming."

His handsome grin disarmed her a moment. She should go pack but she didn't feel she knew enough about him to stay with him yet. And if her daughter was going to be near him for the unforeseeable future…

"In some ways. But growing up that way made me a little naive. I met Evie's father, Ed, when I went to college and moved to Arizona with him. When I got pregnant, he left."

"How does that make you naive?"

Edgar Lovett had lied to her about almost everything about himself. The only thing he hadn't lied about was his college degree. "I should have known he wasn't reliable. I had never met anyone so experienced at duping people. He wasn't at all what he pretended to be. He told me he came from an average family and that his parents were dead."

He also told her that he had never been married before. "I didn't find out until after he left that he was the son of a wealthy Arizona senator and his parents were very much alive. He also was married before we met in college. He divorced his secret wife before I met him and we moved to Arizona."

Hazel didn't know why he had lied. She could only guess he had done so because he was afraid she was using him for his money. The last she had heard, he was living in Florida off his trust fund. Hazel had tried to get child support but he always evaded the attempts. Eventually she gave up and chalked him up as a deadbeat dad, albeit a wealthy one. She didn't have to be told he had abandoned her and Evie because he was incapable of accepting any real responsibility. She wanted to thank him for leaving instead of putting her through a life of struggle with a man like him. She also held a lot of animosity toward him, a man who could have easily afforded to help her out but had not. What kind of person did that? And how had she never seen that about him?

"You weren't naive," Callum said. "I bet he liked you, maybe even loved you, but he must have known you had higher expectations than he could deliver on when it comes to making a family. He misled you because he was probably tired of being identified as a senator's son."

Of course, she thought the same, except her expectations were pretty simple. She didn't require anyone rich or anyone with specific personality traits. She only wanted someone decent. She had told Ed she wanted a good and honest man like her father had been, like so many other men she had grown up around.

"Why bother lying, though, about who he was and about his ex-wife?" Hazel still wanted to know, to this day. "He must have known the truth would come out eventually." Hazel would have left him after learning about his deception.

"You're a beautiful woman, Hazel. Any man would be a fool not to want you."

Ed had lied in order to have her, even if for just a little while. He had never talked about marriage with her, a fact she'd only thought of after he was gone. Then she realized what Callum had just said. Did *he* want her?

"What about you?" she asked, flirting back.

"I've never been married," he said, "and I'm not lying about that." He grinned.

She laughed lightly and briefly, believing him. It was easy to talk with him. Feeling much more comfortable with him, she stopped herself from enjoying this too much. Hadn't she just finished telling him about the biggest mistake she ever made with a man? She would never regret Evie, obviously, but Evie's father was nothing to brag about. She'd rather not wind up having to say the same thing about Callum—or any man. And despite knowing she was biased, she didn't trust anyone wealthy.

"You better get packing," Callum said.

Yes. They'd better pack—rather than play on their attraction to one other.

Chapter 2

Callum leaned against the door frame of Evie's bedroom, watching Hazel pack a bag. She glanced up and saw him.

"Bored?" Her eyes glowed a green hint of her name. Long and dark, finger-tempting wavy hair fell over slender shoulders and framed a remarkably pretty face. Tendrils of that silky splendor curled around melon-shaped breasts. He felt his defenses rise. She had a *daughter*. A really cute one.

"No." He would just rather stare at her. This sudden chemistry threw him off balance.

With a soft smile, she resumed packing.

In just the brief time he had been around Evie—rescuing her, watching her fascination with Kerry and then her bravery in going with the detective—the child had already touched his heart. Now he knew more than ever why he tried so hard to avoid protecting kids. The mothers were another issue completely.

Evie had punched her way through his usual, iron-walled barrier. She was about the same age his daughter would have been, had she and her mother survived. Callum shook off the thoughts. He was better shutting that off, contrary to what Charles said. Despite his cardinal rule never to protect mothers with kids, to leave that up to other bodyguards who didn't share a history similar to his, he could not leave them at the mercy of a man who knew Evie had witnessed him dump a body in a trunk. Now here he was, in Hazel and Evie's apartment, about to take them to the Dales Inn and live with them for however long it took to catch the bad guy.

Hazel finished packing for Evie and went into her bedroom to do the same for herself. Callum followed, she wasn't sure whether out of boredom or because he just enjoyed watching her. The way he did made her acutely aware of him as a man.

"I bet my room is much smaller than the one you sleep in," she said, still self-conscious of his wealth and her bad experience with a man with money.

Callum eyed her peculiarly. "It's a nice apartment. And even though I'm a Colton, I don't dwell on the wealth of my family."

She believed that, but he also must have a sizable bank account, maybe a trust fund or something like that. Just like Ed. That put a sour taste in her mouth.

Taking the bags to the dining area next to the back

entry, she saw Callum go to the mantel above the gas fireplace. She had an electronic photo album there. He gestured with his hand to it.

"These are great."

There were lots of pictures of Evie doing all things Evie. Evie with a toothy smile and mouth smeared with ice cream. Evie holding a bunny rabbit. Evie riding a pony with Hazel. Evie and a friend dressed identically and striking a pose. Hazel and Evie cheek to cheek in a selfie. And so many more. Vacations Hazel had saved for, trips to Disney World and Yellowstone. Them at community events.

As he watched the pictures change, his expression changed. What about these photos put such a look of sadness on his face? She wanted to ask but didn't.

"She's the best thing that ever happened to me," she said instead. "Ed taking off the way he did doesn't even matter anymore. I mean, it did when I was pregnant. What kind of man can abandon their unborn baby?"

Callum didn't say anything, just continued to look at the pictures.

"As soon as Evie was born, everything changed. I didn't care about Ed anymore. She became my world. And she's such a good kid. Even when she was a baby. She didn't cry much, only when she needed something. She slept all night and still does. She rarely has tantrums and when she does, they're over pretty quickly. I'm a lucky mom."

Callum turned to look at her, some of the sadness leaving his eyes. "She's an adorable girl."

"Do you want kids some day?"

"I travel a lot. Usually I'm out of the country on assignments."

He must be some bodyguard. "Do you protect a lot of affluent people?"

"Yes, and high targets for kidnapping in countries where that sort of thing happens."

Dignitaries, politicians and executives for big companies, she supposed.

"I'm only here now to be near my father."

His father had been shot. That must be so difficult, not knowing whether his dad would wake up or not. Callum must be close to his father if he'd changed his work schedule to be by the man's side. She wondered if he regretted helping her, since she obviously was taking time away from his hospital visits.

"If you need to be with him…"

"I'll visit him. I don't have to be with him all the time. I do still have to work, after all. Just not out of state."

Hazel smiled because this was the chattiest he had been since they met.

"You must be close to him," Hazel said, thinking she had made an accurate observation.

"Actually, I'm not," he said, and regret seemed to come over him.

With him out of the country so much, Hazel could see why, but what about when he had been younger? "Was it always that way?"

"Yes. When I was a kid he was always working, and I had my own ideas about what I wanted to do with my life. I knew early on that I never would be an executive like he was." He paused. "Is."

She felt terrible. "If not for me, you would be with him right now."

"No. I was going to visit my brother, but I saw you and…"

And what? He saw her when? Before she had gone into her client's house? And then he had seen that car. She'd changed his plans for the day.

"Which brother?"

"Ace." He shook his head and scratched his forehead in angst. "He's a suspect in my father's shooting. We were never close, either, like with Dad. He followed my dad into the oil business. But I feel for him, you know? He just found out he's not a Colton by blood and there's this clause in the Colton Oil bylaws that says the CEO must be a Colton by blood, and then Dad got shot and everybody thinks he did it—geez, why am I telling you all of this?" He walked toward the back door and the luggage.

Hazel caught up to him and put her hand on his forearm, stopping him from bending to pick up one of the bags. "Hey, it's okay. I like hearing this."

"You like hearing about all my family drama?"

That's all he worried about? She breathed a laugh. "Every family has drama. Why is your brother a suspect?"

"My father had to fire him because of the bylaws. He did it in front of the board, and Ace didn't react well. He threatened my dad."

"How did he threaten him?" With a gun? Had he

said he'd better watch his back or something? Ruin his reputation?

"Ace told Dad he would regret it and stormed out of the room."

"That doesn't mean he shot him."

"I know. I don't think he did, but he shouldn't have threatened him like that, and in front of the board."

Hazel could see he was genuinely concerned for his half brother, despite his claim of not being close to Ace. Just because he had spent a lot of time overseas didn't necessarily mean a family bond didn't exist. Hazel wondered if they were closer than he thought.

"You're easy to talk to," he said after a while, his smile rueful. Did he not open up to anyone? Why had he done so with her?

"Evie doesn't think so."

He chuckled a little. "I saw her arguing with you when you first got to your client's house. I think she does listen to you."

"Like I said, she's a good kid."

"She must have a good mother."

Hazel fell into his eyes, the warm regard there, the attraction. She felt it, too, these underlying sparks that had grown since the moment she saw him.

Once again stopping the sparks, Hazel asked, "So, tell me about this family of yours. You seemed to know that detective, Kerry."

"I come from a large blended family. My father married three times. I have a half sister and two half brothers—including Ace—from the first marriage.

He had none with the second, and my mother had me and my twin sister, Marlowe, plus our brother, Asher. Rafe is my younger adopted brother. He's engaged to Kerry. That's how I know her."

"Ah. She's part of the family now. She's very pretty," Hazel said.

"And smart. And tenacious. She's a rookie but Rafe swears she's as good as a seasoned detective."

"I did get that impression of her, well, short of knowing her, that is. She just had a way about her."

"If anybody can find the man who almost ran you down, she can."

Hazel fell silent, not liking the thought of that. A man capable of hurting or killing another human—especially a child—was a dangerous one, for sure.

"You're a twin?" Hazel asked. "What is that like?"

"We're more like a regular brother and sister, but closer. We were close growing up and still are."

"Are you similar?"

He chuckled at that. "Not at all. Her hair is blonder than mine and she has brown eyes. She's now the CEO of Colton Oil, an executive type. Workaholic." Callum was definitely not an executive type. He was driven in different ways. "But she's pregnant and engaged now, so that will probably change. She's still going to keep her job but she's starting a day-care program."

Hazel seemed to ponder that awhile, as though doubtful that a woman like that could change.

"I technically have one less sibling now—even

though I still consider Ace my half brother. Ace's switch has caused a bit of chaos in the family," he said.

She breathed a tiny laugh at his sarcastic tone. "It sounds dramatic. Who switched him and why?"

"We don't know yet."

"That must be hard for him to face," Hazel said.

He fell silent and Hazel sensed he had given out enough family information for now. Then he just nodded and said, "Yes, it is."

"What made you decide to leave the navy and become a bodyguard?" Hazel asked to change the subject.

"I was getting too old to be a SEAL."

At his short, simplistic reply, she wondered if he didn't want to discuss this. He seemed reluctant to talk about anything personal.

"How old is too old?" she asked anyway.

"I'm thirty-two. Right now, I'm not taking out-of-state assignments, so I can be close to my dad."

"I'm twenty-five," she said. "Have you been married or in any serious relationships?"

She had confessed her failed serious relationship, so that justified her asking the question. "No to marriage. Yes to a relationship, but it didn't work out."

"What happened?"

"It didn't work out," he repeated, turning his head and not looking at her anymore.

She watched the tension on his face for a few seconds, then said, "Sorry. I didn't mean to pry."

"We should get going to the police station. Why don't we go get her and head to the hotel?" Callum said.

She wanted to get to Evie as soon as possible—and slow down whatever was happening between her and Callum.

Waiting for Hazel to finish getting ready to leave, Callum struggled with what her questions had brought to the surface. Shortly after he had left the SEAL team, he had lost Annabel. He never talked about her and their unborn baby. After she died, he had told everyone they'd broken up. He couldn't bear to face the truth and he didn't like people asking him about her. No one had enquired about her in a long time, which probably explained the heavy emotion he felt right now.

When Hazel joined him at the back door, Callum left the apartment, carrying two of her bags with one hand, leaving the other free. He searched the parking area behind the bakery and at first everything seemed quiet. But then he saw someone sitting in a car parked at the end of one of the rows. It was different than the one that had nearly mowed down Evie and Hazel; this one was white with tinted windows. He couldn't see the person inside, but the shape had the form of a man.

Alarmed that someone might try to harm Hazel again, he said, "Go back inside, Hazel."

"What?" Her eyes searched his face beneath lowered eyebrows.

"I need to check out that car over there. Go back inside." He had to keep her safe and she'd be safest in there for now.

Hazel looked out into the parking lot. "Oh, no."

"It might not be anything. Just let me check it out," he said as reassuringly as he could. He didn't mean to frighten her.

She turned and went back inside. He saw her go to the window next to the door and watch.

Callum stepped down the stairs, leaving the bags on the landing by the door. He walked to his truck and started it, then drove closer to the building. There, he waited a few moments. The driver of the other car pulled out of the parking space and drove down the alley toward the street.

Getting out of the truck, Callum went to help Hazel as she came out of the apartment and locked the door. He searched the parking lot and alley, keeping his body between the direction the car had gone and Hazel. He picked up the two bags and followed her down. At the passenger door, he opened that and waited for her to get in, continuing to watch for the mysterious car.

Putting the bags in the back seat, he got behind the wheel and started driving.

At the street he pulled out into traffic, glancing frequently into the rearview mirror. As he suspected, the stranger had waited for them.

Hazel twisted to look behind them. "Is that car following us?"

"Yes."

"Is it the same man?"

"I don't know." Callum turned a corner to see if the stranger would follow.

He did.

Callum turned another corner and the stranger turned, too. He was two vehicles behind them. Callum couldn't see the man clearly.

He decided to drive to the police station. Who in their right mind would try anything in front of a police station? Someone out of their mind…?

Hoping to get a better look at the man, Callum slowed down.

"What are you doing?" Hazel asked in a scared tone.

"I want to see if we can identify him." He watched in the rearview mirror as the vehicle behind him got into the right lane and passed them. The second car moved over next. The white sedan slowed with Callum, maintaining distance. Whoever was driving wouldn't risk being seen up close.

Not wanting to incite the man into drawing a gun or doing anything else that might endanger Hazel, Callum sped up and drove the rest of the way to the station. As they made the turn into the parking lot, the other car drove by. Callum stopped his truck and looked out his window. He saw a man who probably was about six feet tall. He had a hoodie and wore sunglasses—at night—and looked right at him, lights from the dash meagerly reflecting on him.

Callum waited until the white car disappeared from view, having memorized the plate number.

He parked. "Wait for me. Don't get out."

Hazel stayed in the truck and Callum opened the door for her, looking for the white car. Then he put his arm around her and walked with her to the front entrance. Inside, he turned to the glass doors and watched for a few minutes. The car didn't reappear.

He heard Hazel ask for Detective Wilder and turned from the door. A short while later Kerry appeared from a hallway.

"Evie is looking at mugshots," Kerry said. "I thought you both should have a look as well. Right this way." She waved her hand in encouragement.

Callum followed Hazel and Kerry down a hall to an office where Evie was perched on a desk chair that all but swallowed her. Seeing her mother, she hopped down and ran over on her little legs.

"Mommy!"

Hazel picked her up for a hug. "Hi, sweetie. Did you have fun?"

"Yes. The artist is really good. He said he likes his job." Her innocent eyes were wide with excitement.

"Oh, really?"

"And I looked at pictures of bad people."

The kid would probably go down hard when Hazel put her to bed. Who needed sugar when you had such an active imagination? Evie definitely needed a lot of stimulation mentally. She would probably do great in school. He often wondered what his daughter would have been like. Who would she have been? What would her personality have been like? His personality or her mother's?

Callum went over to Kerry and told her about the white car, glad for the distraction. She went to the computer where Evie had been "working" and must have navigated somewhere that would tell her about the car.

"Reported stolen this afternoon," she said.

Damn. The stranger was being very careful. Callum didn't like how he had followed them. He had found where Hazel lived. What if he found them at the inn? He felt enormous pressure to keep Hazel and Evie safe, more so than his usual clients. This seemed more personal.

Before that thought could cause him some heartburn, he went with Hazel to the computer, where Kerry brought up the mugshots. They spent about an hour going through those, but none of them looked familiar. They also couldn't say with any certainty that any of those who had the same type of build might be a potential suspect. Evie's assessment was their best shot at this point.

He'd been so consumed with protecting Hazel and Evie that he hadn't asked Kerry about the progress of the investigation into his father's shooting.

"Hey, have you gotten any further on finding Nan Gelman?" Nan was a nurse who'd been working on the maternity ward at Mustang Valley General Hospital the day Ace had been born—and swapped with another baby. Though the hospital's records had burned, the Coltons were trying to track down Nan to find out what had happened that day.

Kerry made a disgruntled sound. "No. I found a Gelman living in Mountain Valley, but they aren't related to Nan. No one in that family worked at the hospital."

Maybe he'd see what he could dig up. "I might be able to help. My company has resources that you may not have access to."

She brightened. "That would be great."

"Detective Wilder?" Callum looked up and saw an officer in the doorway. "We have a body. It might be related to the near hit and run."

Kerry indicated for Callum and Hazel to follow.

Hazel looked at Callum. "Evie should probably have a tour of the station or something." She should not hear about a dead body.

An officer approached at Kerry's gesture and Evie happily went off to resume her fun-filled day at the police station.

Callum and Hazel went into a conference room, where other detectives had gathered.

"Kerry's here now," the chief of police, Al Barco, said. Fifty-two, mostly bald and with a slight paunch, he had calm, kind green eyes, despite his commanding nature.

And a man started talking through the speakerphone on the long table. "Hi, Kerry. It's Dane Howman."

"Hey, Howman. What have you got for me?"

"A hiker found a body on the banks of a river a few miles from where Evie saw him put in the trunk. Preliminary forensics suggests the cause of death was blunt force trauma to the head. He had a wallet and an ID. It's Nate Blurge."

"I know that guy," one of the other officers in the room said. "He's a wild twenty-six-year-old, been arrested three times for drunk and disorderly conduct. Practically lives at Joe's Bar and always gets into fights."

"Could one of the people he crossed have killed him?" Hazel asked.

"That's a possibility," Kerry said. "It's where we'll start in the investigation."

Hazel looked over at Callum and he could feel her worry. How long would the investigation take? How long would she have to be on high alert?

"I'll find the killer as fast as I can so you and Evie can have your lives back," Kerry said.

Hazel answered with a slight smile that was more of a silent thank-you than anything else. The reassurance didn't alleviate the fear, and Callum's determination to protect them with all the skill he'd gained over the years redoubled.

Rejoining Evie, Hazel flashed back to Callum's reaction when she had asked him about his past relationships. Clearly something bad. It bothered her that he had trouble talking about something personal like that and also made her doubly curious.

Again, both she and Callum added what little information they could to the description of the killer. Right now her daughter was transfixed by Kerry's badge.

"I've booked out one of the two-bedroom suites at the Dales Inn," Callum said.

Hazel looked at him, startled. "You mean…you and me and…" In one suite? "I can't afford that."

"I can. Don't worry."

She kind of did worry, but she decided not to argue. Keeping Evie safe was most important to her. He put his hand over his chest. "I'm a bodyguard. Consider this a professional courtesy. No charge." Now he opened his arms in offering, and oh, what an offering.

She stared at him for long seconds. "Oh, I don't—"

Hazel felt some trepidation at staying with a man she had only just met. Nearly being killed had frightened her but this was all happening so fast. Her routine had been disrupted.

"Actually," Detective Wilder said, removing her badge and handing it to Evie, who took it and felt the top, "Until we find Blurge's killer, I think you should stay at the Dales Inn with Callum."

More than one night? "I don't—"

"I've already offered my services as a bodyguard," Callum cut in again.

Hazel hesitated.

"You're in good hands, Hazel. He is one of the best bodyguards in the country. His company is known for that. They have a solid reputation. You can trust him."

That made her feel marginally better, but it seemed excessive. And with a stranger.

Bodyguard.

She supposed if she thought of him that way…

"You would be my bodyguard?" she asked him.

"Yours and Evie's."

Hazel glanced at Kerry, still uncertain but wavering. "He isn't a policeman." Callum might be six-three and solid muscle, but cops carried guns.

"He's licensed to carry a firearm." Kerry looked at Callum, who moved his jacket aside to reveal the gun in a hip holster.

When Hazel said nothing, just looked over at Evie, Kerry added, "There isn't an officer in this department who wouldn't vouch for him. He does work for a top personal protection agency. Really, I can't say enough good about him."

Hazel put her hand to her forehead. "This is so sudden." She lowered her hand and looked at Evie. The sketch artist handed her a detective shield sticker, which put a big smile on her face. She peeled the back off the sticker and stuck it to the left side of her chest.

"Hey, Detective Evie." Hazel went to her and crouched where she sat at Kerry's desk. Evie beamed, no doubt imagining she was a detective and would go to work just now. "We're going to stay at a hotel tonight. It'll be a vacation."

Evie nodded, looking at Kerry, who had put her badge back on, clearly distracted.

Chapter 3

Having confirmation that the man Evie saw being dumped into a car trunk was dead unsettled Hazel much more than she'd anticipated. Evie had seen the man knocked over the head with a rock. They didn't know if that had killed him. Sure, she had contemplated the possibility, even the likelihood, but having it become fact put them up against a killer. *A killer!*

Callum held the station door for her and Evie, whom she held since her eyes were drooping with the late hour. She saw him scan their surroundings. He put his hand on her back protectively and then his head stopped moving. She followed his gaze and saw a white car drive past the station again and then turn the corner. Apparently the vehicle had been circling the block while they were inside.

"Go and get Kerry," Callum said. "Hurry."

Hazel turned and walked quickly back to the door. When inside, she saw Callum had drawn his gun and was watching the street.

"Is something wrong?"

Hazel heard Detective Wilder and faced her. "The white car that followed us here is still out there. He's going around the block." Just then Hazel spotted the car in front of the station on the street, driving slowly. Callum took cover behind his truck.

Kerry hollered for two other officers and ran out the front door.

"Mommy?" Evie said sleepily.

"It's okay, honey. Go back to sleep." Hazel hoped it would be all right.

Evie rested her head on Hazel's shoulder and closed her eyes. Hazel didn't have time to savor the sight.

Callum opened the station door as Hazel saw Kerry racing away in her car, two other officers following.

"Let's get you out of here," Callum said. "Kerry's on his tail."

She carried Evie out the door.

Callum stayed close to her side with his pistol. At his truck, he opened the back door and guarded them while Hazel put Evie in the car seat he had thoughtfully put in there. Then he opened the passenger door and guarded Hazel again while she got in. Going around to the other side, he got behind the wheel and drove quickly out of the parking lot.

A few minutes later they arrived at the Dales Inn. Hazel knew it was upscale but she had never been this close before. Its grandeur towered before her, the double wooden doors with oval windows welcoming guests to promised luxury. A parking valet gave Callum a ticket.

"Welcome, Mr. Colton," the valet said and then nodded to Hazel. "Ma'am."

"Callum Colton?" a bellboy asked.

"Yes," Callum answered.

"I'll take care of your bags."

"Thank you."

All Hazel had to do was carry a sleeping Evie inside.

The richness of majestic white columns and dark polished stone floors beneath a high, ornately trimmed ceiling engulfed her. Numbly she walked to the reception desk with Callum.

"We're checking in to a two-bedroom suite, please."

Hazel thought about protesting again, but her anxiety over the driver of the white car stopped her. That and Detective Wilder's unwavering praise of Callum's good character.

He took the room keys, then guided Hazel with his hand on her lower back, something that was becoming a habit for him. Strangely, Hazel didn't mind. She wasn't accustomed to a man doting on her the way Callum did. She had always taken care of herself. He might be doing all of that as her bodyguard, but she still liked it. She felt pampered.

They rode the elevator to the top floor with the bellboy and their luggage. Her luggage. Hazel looked at the cart the bellboy had gotten and saw two additional bags. She looked up at Callum in question, Evie's warm breaths touching her neck.

"I arranged for my things to be brought here."

Who had he called? And when? He must have done so while he waited for her to pack. No doubt his family had all kinds of people who did such things for them. Hazel had a funny feeling about that. Ed had hidden his wealth from her, so he had never taken her to places like this, but his lies had hurt. She wouldn't fall so easily for anyone again. Not that she was falling for Callum. He was extremely handsome, that's all. What woman could be immune to that? It was like staring at a beautiful painting, unable to look away until she'd had her fill of the pleasure.

In the posh hallway, Callum stopped at a room door and unlocked it. Then he held the door for Hazel and the bellboy.

"Go ahead and put my bags in the room with one king," Callum said to the bellboy.

"Yes, sir." The bellboy walked down the hall and Hazel followed.

Going into the other bedroom, Hazel drew the covers back on the far queen bed and gently laid Evie on the sheets. She touched her daughter's sleeping face as the bellboy brought in her bags.

"Thanks," she said.

"You're welcome. Enjoy your stay at the Dales

Inn." The young man left and Hazel shut the door before undressing Evie.

It was a bit of a challenge to get her daughter into pj's but she finally succeeded without waking her. The poor kid was exhausted.

Hazel unpacked both of their bags, hanging some clothes and putting some in drawers. She put Evie's toys on one of the chairs in front of the draperies and then spread Evie's favorite soft blanket over her. Leaning down, she kissed her daughter's forehead.

Going out to the main room, she saw Callum on his phone, standing between a four-seater dining table and a sectional that faced a gas fireplace with a TV over it. He talked to someone as he faced the corner windows, Mustang Valley town lights sparkling outside.

There were some things on the table, a computer and other equipment. As she neared, she saw three GPS tracking devices, several USB drives. Some devices looked high tech, others had tiny screens, and she saw bulletproof vests, one small enough to fit Evie. Now she knew why he had two bags.

"All right. Keep me informed," he said and then disconnected.

Hazel went to the four bar stools at a marble-topped kitchen island with a sink in the middle. Three pretty orange-gold pendants hung from the ceiling. A four-burner gas stove with a microwave above was on the other side, and there were cabinets on both sides. It even had a pantry.

She put her hands on the back of one of the chairs.

"This is very nice. I'm more of a two- or three-star hotel kind of girl." Not a fiver.

He chuckled. "We need the space and you need a kitchen. Think of it as a home away from home."

Hazel had told him she was a chef on the way to the Dales Inn but not much else. Leaving the chair, she went around the island and began going through the cabinets. The kitchen was fully stocked with all the equipment she would need. "The only things missing are food and spices."

"Make a list and I'll have that delivered in the morning."

With the snap of a finger he'd do that? "Then I'll pay you."

"No, you won't. I want you to relax and have as much semblance of your normal routine as possible. Don't worry about anything other than doing your job and taking care of Evie. I'll do the rest."

Finished checking out the kitchen, seeing it had pretty much everything, she walked to the impressive windows. Mustang Valley looked bigger than she had always thought of it from here.

"Why are you doing this?" she asked.

She heard him walk up behind her and stop beside her. "I was there when the man tried to run you over."

He had already indicated as much, but she wanted to know why he was here with her. Why had he offered his services, free of charge?

"Why this?" She turned as she swept her arm out into the room, facing him. "Why is it so important for you to help us?"

She met his incredibly blue eyes while he considered his reply.

"I don't know," he finally said. "When I first saw you, I had no intention of going out to meet you, but then I saw that car with the driver and instincts kicked in. This is what I do, Hazel."

That sounded truthful enough. Why, then, did she have this feeling that it was more personal than that?

"Kerry called. She lost the white car," Callum said, pulling her thoughts elsewhere. "She said the driver must know the town well. Otherwise he might not have gotten away as easily as he did."

Hazel bit her lower lip in consternation. The killer had gotten away. Where was he now? Lurking outside? Did he already know they were here? Picturing Evie's sweet sleeping face, she released her lip with a long sigh. If the killer knew the town well, he'd know the Dales Inn was the only hotel in Mustang Valley.

Feeling as though someone could see them through the windows, she went to stand by the dining table.

Callum went to the other side. "I sleep light, so don't worry. And if you have any lingering doubt as to why I'm doing this, now you shouldn't. I couldn't leave a dog in danger like this."

She believed that his work was second nature to him, but she still thought there was more to him than that, more that drew him to her and Evie, maybe even something he hadn't acknowledged himself. Yet.

Looking down at all the items on the table, she

pointed to the vests. "I take it we're going to be wearing those?"

"Whenever we leave the inn. They're knife- and bulletproof and made with poly-cotton netting that breathes to keep you cool or warm, depending on the weather. You can wear them underneath your clothes. They're comfortable."

Very high tech. And she would feel so much better knowing Evie would be protected as best as she could.

"What will you do with the USB drives?" she asked.

"Some are listening devices, others are cameras. One is for deleted file recovery." He gestured to the USB devices. "We'll put a GPS in your car, purse and Evie's backpack. They all have extended battery life."

Hazel couldn't bear to think she or Evie might be abducted, but Callum would know where they were if it happened. He wasn't taking any chances. She couldn't imagine they would need to recover any deleted files in order to find the killer. Maybe that was another precautionary measure Callum had taken.

"I've got some night vision goggles and extra guns and ammo in the bag. I'll keep those in a safe place."

Out of Evie's curious hands. That was comforting. Hazel met his eyes, thinking she could never get tired of doing so. She could stare at them for an hour and float on a cloud of infatuation. How many other handsome men had she seen and not had such a strong reaction? She had been quite attracted to Ed, but she had never felt this way with him. Callum might be ruggedly gorgeous but Hazel didn't think he'd be a good match for her.

What made a good match? She did not know him at all, at least, not very well. He physically attracted her. What would she do with that? What if she had no control over what was between them?

Why are you doing this?
Why is it so important for you to help us?

Those two questions that Hazel had asked kept repeating in his mind and he couldn't shut off the voice. He was tired of hearing it. Mostly he was tired of wondering why and feeling somewhere deep inside that he already knew the answers.

He opened the drawer of the built-in desk next to the kitchen, looking for a notepad and pen. Hazel had gone to sit on the sectional. It was getting late but she needed to give him a list of kitchen necessaries so he could have everything she needed by morning.

He had been truthful when he had told her instinct had taken over. Instinct had made him walk across the street to check on the mysterious car. He hadn't really thought much beyond that, but now here he was, guarding a woman and her child.

Finding a notepad and pen, he brought it to Hazel and sat beside her. "Here you go. Make your list."

She tapped the pen lightly against her lower lip awhile before finally beginning to write down ingredients.

Callum studied her profile, sloping nose and full lips. Long lashes low over hazel-green eyes. He let his gaze travel lower, noticing a button on her white blouse had come loose and exposed more of her cleavage. She was a stunning woman.

He turned his attention to her growing list.

"Do you have regulars?"

"Yes. I'm a personal chef," she answered without pausing in her writing.

Leaning over he started reading the list. "Are the ingredients all meat and potatoes?"

Smiling she slid a glance toward him. "No. Some are chicken and mashed potatoes."

He chuckled. "I could do that job."

"I also have clients who want things like shrimp and scallop scampi. Roasted chicken au jus. Seafood-stuffed salmon. Steak. Lobster. Vegetable dishes. Fruit."

He would like to try a few of her concoctions. But since he barely knew her, he didn't mention it.

"What made you decide to become a chef?" he asked.

She smiled softly. "My mother cooked all the time. I grew up with delicious smells wafting from the kitchen."

"You never told me about your family. You know all about mine and I know nothing about yours." That wasn't fair. He felt safe asking her, not too personal.

"Not much to tell," she said. "My parents are both from Pagosa Springs, Colorado. They knew each other in high school but didn't get together until after college. My brother is a cop and lives in Phoenix with his wife's family."

"I'm sure there is more to tell than that."

She smiled in that soft way again. "Are you looking for drama?"

"You did say every family has it." He was starting to love this banter.

She laughed once. "Um…let's see…well, there was the time when my brother skipped school to smoke pot with his friends. My parents flipped. They were afraid he would drop out of school or be kicked out and his whole future would be in ruins. But it turned out he just went through a phase. He rebelled for a year and then got his grades back up and went on to college."

To become a cop. Her family drama paled in comparison to his. "What about you? Did you ever rebel?"

"No. I was never good at math or the sciences, but I managed a B average. Art was my forte. I oil painted, drew in lead and colored pencils. My paintings were often displayed in the school hall outside the art room. My parents worried I'd never make a comfortable income. They sat me down for a talk my senior year and said, 'Hey, look, you might not be able to support yourself.' Their way of saying they were convinced I'd be the clichéd starving artist." She laughed. "I suppose I am still, in some ways."

He liked that she smiled and laughed so much. He smiled and laughed, too, at least he thought he did.

"You were an artist and became a chef," he said. "How did you go from one to the other?"

That made her think a moment, tipping her head up a bit, eyes lifting in search of an answer. He could see the flecks of green glowing.

"I think the talk with my parents influenced me," she said. "I went to college for interior design, but one of my optional classes was culinary. That's what changed everything. I loved the art of making plates look like colorful, abstract paintings. And then I fell in love with flavors and aromas. I dropped out of college after the first semester and went to culinary school."

She must have a knack for it, since she was so young and already striving for success. "You're self-employed. That's quite an accomplishment."

"I only recently went out on my own. I did my externship at Flemming's, a renowned restaurant here in Arizona."

"I've heard of it. Where did you go to school that got you that kind of externship?" he asked.

"The Culinary Institute of America."

He whistled. How had she been able to afford that? He didn't know the exact tuition but did know it was among the best culinary arts schools in the country, if not the world.

"My parents saved for my college education. They gave me almost half and I took out student loans for the rest. That and the externship got me my first job at a place called Carolyn's Kitchen. It was an upscale, home-style restaurant. I helped them spiff up their menu and some of the meals I created gave me the idea to go out on my own. Jasmine, the owner of the bakery, lets me cook in her kitchen when I have a big order or several all at once. I cook after the bakery closes at two."

She didn't appear to make a ton of money, living in the small apartment, but she had to be getting along just fine, making a decent income to support herself and Evie. Callum admired that. He admired ambition in anyone. Working hard was rewarding. It didn't matter if the hard work made a person wealthy. If Callum hadn't been born a Colton, he wouldn't be wealthy. He made a good income, more than an average bodyguard, but nothing approaching what his father made.

"What's your favorite food?" Hazel asked, handing him the notepad.

Taking it, his fingers brushed hers. She gave him the pen as their eyes met.

"Seafood. Clams. Scallops. That scallop recipe sounded really good."

"Clams. I could make you an outstanding clam dinner. We'd have to make something else for Evie. She doesn't like seafood."

"Does any kid?"

She took the pen and paper back and jotted down some more ingredients. Then she handed the list back to him. He put it on the coffee table.

"What are you going to make me?"

"Linguine with white clam sauce."

"Mmm." He couldn't wait for that. Spending time with her in the kitchen, too. Doing anything with her.

He liked being with her. "How much time do you need to cook tomorrow?"

"Five or six hours."

Taking out his phone, he took a picture of the list then texted it to one of his agency's best personal staff and asked to have everything by nine in the morning. Patsy Cornwall responded a few seconds later. She was a night owl. Callum could always depend on her.

"Just like that, we'll get all the ingredients?" Hazel sounded amazed.

"Just like that. Patsy is paid very well for her services."

"Is she some kind of concierge?"

"She's a personal assistant. She works from home and runs errands for us when we need it. We all keep her pretty busy."

"Nice. Lucky me." Hazel gave him the pleasure of one of her soft smiles and the color of her eyes spellbound him.

She moved her head a fraction closer, as though she couldn't help it, stopping short and looking into his eyes.

Callum lifted his hand and placed his palm against her cheek, then, nearly involuntarily, pressed his mouth to hers. She immediately responded, her warm lips melding with his and sparking much more carnal urges. The intensity of sensations just a kiss caused in him made him withdraw.

She opened her eyes and he found himself transfixed again. He had only known her for about ten hours. With all that had happened, he felt he had known her a lot longer.

"I should get some sleep. Tomorrow is going to be a busy day," she said.

"Right. Yes." He stood with her, seeing her smooth her hair and press her lips together as though she could still feel him kissing her.

He walked behind her toward their bedrooms, she veering to the right and he to the left. When she reached her door, she slowed and looked at him. A moment of electrified attraction passed between them before she disappeared from view.

Callum entered his room and closed the door. While he undressed and got into bed, he imagined what it might be like to be naked with Hazel. On his back, he folded his arm under his head and stared at the dark ceiling, the passionate urges subsiding as the reality of starting something romantic with her set in. Hazel, single mother of Evie, an adorable little girl who reminded him of what his own daughter might have been.

Daughter. He had never formed that word since his girlfriend died. And now an intense sense of dread came over him. Dread and a horrible, defenseless feeling that swirled in his stomach.

Okay. He had gotten himself into this mess. He would treat it like any other job. Watch out for Hazel and Evie. Get them through what they had witnessed. Catch the bad guy. Move on to the next client. No more kissing Hazel.

Chapter 4

When Hazel woke, she didn't immediately know where she was. She had been so exhausted, she'd slept deeply. Now, pushing the covers off, she sat up to be surrounded by the luxury of the Dales Inn room. With white, brown and splashes of color in paintings, the room was immaculate and quiet. She stood and saw Evie had already gotten up.

Checking the time, she saw it was almost eight. Going to the door, she cracked it open and heard Evie chattering happily away. Assured her daughter was fine, Hazel hopped in the shower. Remembering kissing Callum, she tipped her face up into the spray, feeling him all over again. She'd had trouble falling asleep last night because of that. She couldn't even blame him, though, since she was the one who had leaned in. She had been so entranced by him, by his eyes and every feature of his face. The sound of his voice and the things they had talked about, the connection between them.

She dressed in gray slacks and a black blouse and left the room, hearing voices.

"I love strawberries."

"I can seen that you do," Callum said.

"I *looove* strawberries," Evie repeated.

Evie sat at the dining room table with a huge plate of strawberry crepes in front of her. The dish dwarfed her head and upper torso, just her shoulders cleared the height of the tabletop.

"What are you doing to my daughter?"

Callum looked up from the table, where he arranged two breakfast plates that still had silver covers on them.

He chuckled. "She said she was starving. I hope this is okay with you. I sort of winged it by ordering room service." He pointed to the plate at Evie's right. "That's yours. I'm glad I didn't have to wake you before it got cold."

"More than fine. I'm starving, too." She sat next to Evie and lifted the cover.

"It's a Santa Fe skillet," Callum said. "Wheat toast and fruit for sides. Evie picked it out for you. She said you liked food like that. There was a picture on the room service menu."

She did like food like this. Evie knew she loved green chilies.

He poured her a cup of steaming coffee. "Cream or sugar?"

"Yes, please, just creamer."

He handed her two small containers of creamer and she went about adding both to her coffee as Callum sat across from her and removed the silver cover from his plate. He had gotten a ham and cheese omelet with rye toast.

"Do you eat out a lot?" she asked.

With a bite of food, he nodded. Then after swallowing, added, "Bachelor."

She and Evie rarely ate out, but why would they, when Hazel cooked for a living?

"Evie told me the last man you were with was a… what did you call it?" He turned to Evie.

"A nerd." Evie giggled before shoveling another bite of crepe into her mouth.

"Evie was worried you were falling for him," Callum said.

Hazel saw his questioning look. She had dated James for a few weeks. She didn't like talking about him.

"Well, Evie, you're awfully chatty this morning," she said.

Evie giggled. "Cal-em is funny."

"Why is he funny?"

"I don't know. He's funny. He's not a nerd."

Gaze running over his shoulders and chest, Hazel had to agree. When she met his eyes, the same tingles of sexual awareness assaulted her, just as they had last night.

"Who is this nerd? He must have been important to you if you let him spend time with Evie."

"He didn't think Mommy was smart. He called her stupid once."

Callum's lower jaw dropped. "What?"

"She told him to leave. Except she used a bad word."

Hazel remembered the sting of James's condescension all too well. Just when she had begun to trust him, he'd turned on her. He had made her feel the same awful sense of betrayal that Ed had.

"He had a PhD in economics," she said. "Apparently he was very proud of that."

"Why did he call you stupid?" Callum asked, sounding incredulous.

"We were talking about retirement. I didn't have anything put away at the time. My sole focus was Evie, taking care of her, saving for her college, making sure she has medical insurance and good clothes and shoes and healthy food. It escalated to an argument and he called me stupid. He said I didn't know arithmetic or anything about science and all I did know was how to cook."

As she talked Callum's brows gradually rose with each insult. "The man is clearly mad. And completely blinded by his own self-interests."

She wasn't sure she could have said that better.

"Just because you're more inclined to the arts doesn't make you stupid," Callum said. "A person doesn't have to be a genius in math or any of the hard sciences to be intelligent." He shook his head. "I can't believe anyone would say that to another person."

"I thought he was a decent man, just like Ed." She glanced at Evie. The little girl didn't yet understand what had happened between her mother and father, but some day Hazel would have to have that talk with her. She wouldn't disparage Ed's character, just state the facts. What she dreaded most was that Evie would feel her father never loved her, even though he hadn't. He didn't. He didn't care about Evie. He didn't even know her name. Maybe she could tell Evie someday that her father never knew her, but that if he ever did, or took the time to, then he would love her.

When Hazel turned back to Callum, she saw he had caught her meaning. She was no good at assessing men, at predicting their characters. She had always been trusting, had had no reason not to be, having been surrounded by good people, raised in a stable family.

"I've always thought relationships were based on trial and error," he finally said. "Sometimes the trials go well but you learn the person isn't right for you and you respectfully part ways. Sometimes the trials go badly and end up a mistake. But eventually, with a little luck, you find a person who works."

Works? He sounded as though he believed what he said, or had at one point. "What kind of trials have you had?"

"Ones where I learned something, and some that were a mistake."

"What did you learn?" She'd start with the easier question to answer.

His shrewd mind must be at work. He eyed her

with subtle suspicion mixed with intrigue, perhaps, and then his head cocked ever so slightly.

"Too personal?" she asked, half teasing.

A one-sided grin was his initial response, then he said, "I learned that some women are more interested in their own gain, and others aren't certain enough about what kind of man they're searching for or don't care as long as he is kind and capable of providing. I've learned those kinds of women aren't for me."

Oh, my. This man knew what he wanted. He sounded so candid. She didn't doubt he had learned what he claimed, but what about the mistakes? Maybe there had been only one.

"What about your mistakes?" she dared to ask.

Going still, he just looked at her.

A knock on the door interrupted. Callum went to the door and in came carts of groceries and supplies.

"Whoa!" Evie exclaimed, holding a sticky fork and sporting a strawberry-stained mouth. She put her utensil down, prongs up, on the table, watching the assistant roll bags of food into the suite.

"I'll help put all of this away," Patsy said. A woman of average height with wavy brown hair and blue eyes, she had an energy about her that radiated efficiency.

Evie got off the chair. "Are we going to cook, Mommy?"

"I'm going to cook. You're going to go take a bath." She stood. "Come on. I'll get you started."

Hazel saw the assistant begin to put groceries

away and Callum lending a hand. The refrigerator would be bursting by the time they finished.

In their en suite, Hazel started the bath and then went to Evie's stash of toys and found her floating Barbie boat and doll. Returning to the bathroom, she discovered Evie had removed her clothes and stepped into the filling tub.

Seeing Hazel had her favorite toys, she smiled and reached up for them. "Yes."

Hazel laughed with the affection that filled her. She handed her daughter the toys and Evie went instantly into playtime mode. Leaving the door open so she could hear her if anything happened, Hazel left the room and saw that Patsy had gone and Callum was removing cooking pans from a box. Patsy must have brought them, since the inn only had a minimal collection.

"You're going to help?" Hazel asked, going to the sink to wash her hands.

"I wouldn't want to ruin anything. I'll keep you company. I have nothing else to do until I make all your deliveries."

"I make the deliveries. It's good PR."

"No, I'll make them. You stay here, where you and Evie will be safe."

She had spoken without thinking, distracted with getting ready to cook for a few hours.

"I'll tell your customers Evie is sick and you sent me instead," he said. "I'll be charming. You won't lose any business."

Was he a good liar? She wished she could be there

to hear him so she could make that assessment. Then again, she was never any good at detecting falsehoods.

While Callum made a call to Kerry to ask her to post an officer outside the inn while he made deliveries, Hazel decided to start with the pork chops. Brining them first, she felt Callum observing her work. While the chops soaked for thirty minutes, she moved on to the chicken and broccoli. Turning on the oven, she put the meat in a bowl, seasoned it and drizzled the cutlets with olive oil. All the while she contemplated picking up her conversation with Callum. She was beyond curious over what mistakes he had made. She knew there was one, probably a big one that he had trouble talking about.

She placed the broccoli on one baking pan and the chicken on another, then put both into the oven. Next, she began preparing spaghetti sauce, cooking the meat first.

"Mommy," Evie called from the room. She must be finished with her bath.

"I'll watch the meat." Callum took her place at the stove.

Hazel hurried to the room and helped Evie dry off, giving her hair a rub with the towel. "Get dressed, honey."

Evie went to the drawers where Hazel had placed her clothes and began digging through them. She'd make a mess and take forever to find something she liked. For the last year Evie had insisted on dressing herself. Usually she didn't match very well, but she always looked cute.

Back in the kitchen, Hazel took over at the stove, Callum moving aside. He leaned his hip on the counter and again Hazel became aware of his more than casual observation of her. She resumed preparing the meals.

A while later, Evie emerged from the room, half skipping her way toward them, her hair an utter mess. In the kitchen, she stopped next to Hazel.

"Mommy." She lifted the brush.

Callum stepped around Hazel and took the brush. "I'll do it. Your mother is working."

Picking her up, Callum took her to the other side of the kitchen island and sat her on a tall stool. Hazel had a great view of her as he began to brush her long hair. Evie brushed her Barbie doll's hair at the same time.

"How long are you going to be with my mommy?" Evie asked Callum.

"I don't know, Evie. It depends on how long it takes to catch that bad man," he said, struggling with a tangle.

His big body and manly hands running the brush through a five-year-old's hair touched Hazel for some reason.

"Are you and Mommy going to be friends after?"

Callum's hand paused in brushing her hair. "Do you want me to be?"

Evie shrugged. "Are you working for her?"

"Yes, I am."

"But you're her friend, too."

It was Hazel's turn to pause in her task. Why had her daughter asked such a question?

"We just met yesterday, but yes, she is a friend." Callum looked at Hazel with a grin, clearly enjoying this conversation. He began brushing again.

"Mommy needs more boy friends." She tipped her head up. "I don't have a daddy."

"You do have a daddy, Evie, he just isn't here," Hazel said. Why was her daughter bringing this up now? She wasn't prepared to have this talk so soon.

"Where is he?" Evie resumed brushing her doll's hair.

"He...wasn't interested in being with me."

"Does he know about me?"

"Yes, but he has never met you." Hazel glanced at Callum, who looked back at her somberly.

Evie lowered the doll and looked at Hazel. "Why not?"

"He left me, Evie. It had nothing to do with you."

"But...doesn't he want to meet me?"

"You're awfully inquisitive for a young girl," Hazel said.

"Some people aren't prepared to raise kids," Callum said. "Sometimes they aren't ready until much later in life. He doesn't know you, but if he did, he would see what a special girl you are."

Hazel's heart burst with appreciation and awe that, without prompting, Callum had told Evie something similar to what she had thought she would say.

"Do you have a daddy?"

"I do. We aren't very close, though."

That had surprised Hazel when he'd told her before. He seemed so concerned over his father. If they weren't close, why weren't they? Evie had looked up at him with his answer and Hazel could see a connection forming. Did Evie relate her lack of a relationship with her father to his?

"Do you have any kids?" Evie asked, a fountain of questions.

Callum finished brushing her hair and put down the brush. "No."

"Are you going to?"

Hazel watched him tense up. She wondered—if it had been anyone other than a child asking, would he have retorted something to stop this grilling? She also began to worry about Evie's unabashed curiosity about Callum. She seemed to have taken a liking to him rather quickly, which might not be a good thing.

"Evie, that's enough. We barely know Callum. It isn't polite to ask so many personal questions," Hazel said, sure that Evie's Curious George mode was too much for Callum.

Evie's lower lip puffed out a little in a pout, but then she brightened quickly enough. "Can I go watch cartoons?"

"Sure," Hazel said.

Callum helped her get the television on and tuned to the right channel and then returned to the kitchen island. Hazel had put the chicken into the oven and gone to work on the chops, getting a pan ready to sear them.

She busied herself in the kitchen for the next few hours. Callum had gone into the living room to watch television with Evie. The two were getting chummy in there. Callum had found a good family movie that adults could enjoy.

Hazel began putting food into microwavable containers and then into the refrigerator. Her customers could freeze what they wouldn't use in the next day or two. Instant, delicious meals for busy workers or the elderly.

"Will you write down the addresses?" Callum asked. "The officer is outside. I checked."

While that was reassuring, he couldn't keep her penned up in here until the killer was caught. She had a life to live. But dragging Evie around with them wasn't a wise idea, either. Damn that stranger. He was taking her freedom from her. She needed her freedom, but she was no fighter like Callum. Better that he did what he could. He was right. She and Evie were safer here.

"You're doing an awful lot to keep us safe," she said.

Callum stepped closer to her. He put his fingers beneath her chin. Heat coursed through her as she tried to figure out why he had touched her this way.

"It's more than wanting you safe, Hazel. I have a personal reason for doing so. You see, I normally don't take the cases involving women and children. Protecting them. It just so happens that I fell into protecting you and Evie and now I cannot turn my back. I have to see this through."

He seemed to be trying to make her understand why it was so important to him that she stay here in their suite. She still didn't get it. He had to see this through…but why *him*? Why didn't he take cases involving women and children? Why make such a pledge?

"I can't explain it right now. All I ask is you trust me," he said.

After a moment of stunned perplexity, she nodded. She wouldn't press him now, but the need to know would gnaw at her until he told her everything. If he ever did…

Mystified over how close he had come to telling Hazel his darkest secret, Callum began loading the containers of food into his truck. What really got him was that he had felt as though he *could* tell her. And that maybe a huge burden might be lifted if he did. Maybe Charles was right. Maybe keeping all of that bottled up was doing more harm than good.

Memories of when he had first met Annabel flooded him. He had been at a home improvement store looking at wood-saw blades to remodel his bathrooms. Annabel had been looking at the drills. He'd found that interesting. It wasn't every day a guy saw a woman buying tools, unless it was for her man. Callum hadn't seen a ring, so he had gone over to her.

"Are you a carpenter?" he had asked.

Her head had come up and she looked at him for endless seconds. She had long dark hair and dark eyes. Very beautiful.

"No." She had held up a drill in her hand. "Replacing old doors in my house."

"You don't hire out for that?"

"Why? Because I'm a woman?"

From that moment on, he had fallen hard for her. They talked for hours. They spent quiet times together, just comfortable in each other's company. Callum had thought they had the makings of something special, but he hadn't had time to really get to know her. They had only begun to explore. They hadn't been together long before—

He could not let his mind dwell any more on that. A deep sorrow penetrated his usual wall of carefully crafted indifference. He finished putting the food in the truck and closed the door.

As he walked to the rear of the truck on the way to the other side, he spotted a black SUV. That in and of itself didn't alert him, but the man sitting in the driver's seat did. The guy was just sitting in a vehicle.

The passenger window rolled down and he barely noticed the muzzle of a gun before diving for cover. He just made it around the side of his truck before bullets hit the bumper and rear tailgate.

He drew his own weapon and inched up enough to see the shooter. He took aim and fired before ducking as more bullets hit his truck. Hearing the SUV's engine rev and tires squeal, Callum tried again to shoot the driver. He had to take cover again as the SUV raced by and bullets pummeled the truck.

When the volley subsided, Callum got into the truck from the passenger side and crawled behind the wheel, fleetingly seeing a couple crouching at the entrance of the inn, one of them with a cellphone to his ear. Starting the truck, he peeled out of the parking space and chased after the SUV. He veered in and out of traffic, seeing the vehicle several car lengths ahead.

The shooter turned a corner. Callum was slowed by traffic and when he made the turn, he didn't see the SUV. He searched side streets as he weaved, earning honks from a few drivers. Looking left, he spotted the SUV and nearly sideswiped an oncoming car as he swerved into the turn. He gave the truck full gas, no cars in his way, and careened into another turn. The SUV had vanished again, but Callum saw an alley. Swerving into the turn, he gained on the SUV. The shooter flung out into traffic on a busier street. Other traffic veered out of the way as the driver maneuvered around them, Callum not far behind.

There was no plate on the SUV.

The shooter craned back to fire his weapon again and bullets struck Callum's windshield. He crouched low and stuck his pistol out his window, firing back. The shooter drove erratically and made a sharp right turn, causing a delivery truck to brake hard and swerve.

With the delivery truck in his way Callum had to stop and then drive around. People scattered on the sidewalk. The SUV had distance on him again. The shooter turned a corner about a block and a half ahead.

But when Callum reached the street, he didn't see the SUV. He searched until he reached another road. He checked both ways, but the SUV was nowhere in sight. Making a guess, he drove left. A few minutes later it became apparent he would not find the shooter.

His cell rang. Seeing it was Hazel, he answered.

"Are you all right?" she asked. "There are a bunch of police out front and someone said there was a shooting."

"I'm okay. Stay in the room. The shooter came after me. I tried to chase him but he got away."

She was silent for a while. "I'll stay in the room. Be careful."

"I'll be back soon." He liked the concern for his welfare in her voice but not her worry. He thought about rushing back to Hazel, but she was safe in the inn, which had solid security. There were security cameras everywhere and a security team. That was probably why the shooter had waited outside. He knew if he tried to go inside and kill anyone, he'd be captured on video. Besides, the police were there now.

He called Kerry.

She answered on the second ring.

"The killer tried to shoot me just now," Callum said.

"I heard."

He explained what had happened and that he didn't get a plate number this time.

"Well, we can pretty much assume he's stealing vehicles to avoid identification," she said.

"He's getting bold. He waited for us outside the inn. How did he know we were there? How did he find out so fast?"

"Mustang Valley isn't very big. Dales Inn is the

only hotel in town. I'm sure he deduced you and Hazel would go there if you weren't at her place."

"What about the ranch?"

"I'm sure he checked there, too."

Callum ran his fingers through his hair as he drove to the address of the first delivery.

"I'll put out a BOLO on the SUV and check for any reported stolen vehicles," Kerry said. "Be careful."

Nobody had to tell him that. Ending the call, he gathered the bag with all the containers for Emily Watson, one of Hazel's elderly clients. With glasses on a chain, her silver hair in stiff curls and a face covered in peach fuzz, Emily smiled her welcome in a floral house dress. Callum was immediately charmed.

She glanced down at the bag he held. "Where is Hazel?"

"She's not feeling well so I'm making her deliveries for her. My name is Callum."

"Come in, come in." Emma stepped aside and checked him out. "My, my, aren't you a handsome fellow."

Callum entered the older Victorian, dark wood floors creaking, letting her comment go.

Emily shut the door and led him into the kitchen. "Go ahead and put them in the freezer. That's what Hazel always does. I still have one of her delicious meals in the refrigerator and with it just being me, that lasts a few days. My Irwin passed a few years ago and the kids don't come around as often as I'd like."

She must be lonely and starved for adult conversation. Callum opened the freezer drawer and began rearranging the contents to make room for a week's worth of meals.

"Irwin was an engineer and retired a vice president of his department," Emma said. "He was a good provider. What is it that you do, Mr...?"

"Colton. I'm a personal protection officer." That always sounded more palatable than *bodyguard*.

"Oh, you're a security guard?" Emily asked, going to a glass-faced cabinet. "Would you like something to drink?"

She didn't recognize his last name. Maybe it was her age. "No, thank you. No, I'm not a security guard."

Emma filled a glass with tap water. "Hazel never told me about you. She and I have such lovely talks when she's here."

Callum imagined Emily talked anyone's ear off when they visited. Plumbers. Electricians. Maybe the mail carrier. And her kids when they came over.

"She is such a dear," Emily said. "I know she doesn't have to stay when she delivers my meals, but she does. She genuinely cares about me. She's become a friend of mine even if she doesn't consider me one of hers."

"I'm sure she does."

"She's a very good chef." Emily patted her tummy, which wasn't protruding much at all. "She felt so bad for leaving that job of hers, but she belongs on her own."

"She felt bad?" Hazel hadn't mentioned that.

"Oh, yes. Hazel is such a conscientious person. She wouldn't hurt a flea. She worried about the owner of that restaurant…what was it called? Carolyn's Kitchen. She and Carolyn were good friends. Carolyn didn't want her to leave but Hazel followed her heart, and good thing she did. She's going to be very successful someday. You wait and see."

"She already seems to be."

"It's nice to see that she's finally found a husband and father for Evie. I'm going to have to ask her why she didn't tell me."

Husband and father? Callum stood, finished putting the containers into the freezer, feeling a lump form in his throat. He swallowed.

Emily smiled fondly at him, making him more uncomfortable. "I always knew it would only be a matter of time. Hazel is so pretty and nice. And her daughter is sweet as can be. But I'm sure you already know that."

"Hazel and I aren't married," he said.

Emily waved her hand in dismissal. "You don't have to get married to be a family these days. Look at Kurt Russell and Goldie Hawn. They're a model of how healthy families survive without being taken down by old traditions."

Her refreshing outlook did little to calm his inner turmoil. Being a part of Hazel's family would bring heavy responsibility. Callum would go crazy worrying for their well-being. His line of work brought plenty of danger. The people he protected clients against might go after his family to get to him.

Emily stepped closer and gave his forearm a few pats. "If you aren't romantic with her yet, you will be. I'm good at reading people and you seem like a decent man. Unlike Evie's father. Hazel says she won't go for the gorgeous and rich types ever again." She observed him critically. "You're gorgeous, but I bet you aren't rich. Bodyguards don't make that much, do they?"

What did she mean by that? Hazel had told her she would never be with anyone wealthy?

"I don't make millions protecting my clients, but I make more than average," he said, not going into any details of the company that employed him—or the fact that he was a Colton. This woman was already making him talk too much.

"I better get back to Hazel and Evie." He began to back off.

"Yes, I'm sure they are anxiously waiting your return. It was very nice to meet you, Mr. Colton." Emily's face sobered as though something dawned on her. "Colton. You're Payne Colton's son?"

"I am." Maybe she wouldn't be so quick to pair him with Hazel now.

"I heard about the shooting. Who would do such a thing? And how is he doing? Is he going to survive?"

"We don't know yet." Reminded of his father, he planned to go see him in the morning.

Emily's mouth pursed as though mulling over

something troubling. "What I said before about Hazel not seeing anyone rich… I didn't mean…"

Callum held his hand up. "Don't worry about it. Hazel and I aren't together that way."

"Are you working for her? She hired you? Is she in danger?"

"Evie witnessed a crime. I'm staying with her until the suspect is captured."

Emily put her hand over her mouth with a sharp inhale. Lowering her hand, she asked, "Is she all right?"

"Yes."

"Because you're watching over her." Emily smiled. "You might come from wealth but you're not the same ilk as Edgar. I can tell."

Right. Because she was good at reading people. Maybe that was true. When a person lived as long as Emily had, they grew wise. She had no magical insight. And Callum would not give credence to anything she had shared with him today. Even if he secretly wanted to.

Evie wouldn't eat her vegetables. Hazel had neared her limit of tolerance just when Callum reentered the suite. She quelled the surge of gladness seeing him made her feel. Evie, on the other hand, did nothing to hide hers. She jumped off the chair and ran to him with a squeal and a loud "Cal-em!"

He bent as she crashed into him, tiny arms going around his torso, reaching his sides and no farther. Callum lifted her and carried her to the table.

"Mommy and I made cookies today. Chocolate."

"Chocolate chip," Hazel corrected.

"And we watched *Frozen*."

"For the thirtieth time," Hazel quipped.

"Hectic day?" Callum asked her.

Seeing his teasing grin, she said, "Evie wanted to go for ice cream. I've been arguing with her all afternoon. Now she won't eat her vegetables."

Callum put Evie down. "Why don't you go do as your mother says? You don't want to grow up short and puny, do you?"

Hazel had to hide a laugh.

"What's puny?" Evie asked.

"Littler than everyone else your age. Go on."

"Will you read to me first?"

Hazel rolled her eyes behind her daughter's back. What a manipulator. But even at her worst, Evie was the most precious thing ever.

"After you do as your mother says and finish your dinner."

With a pout and much slower steps back to the table, Evie climbed up onto the chair and picked up her fork. As she began eating, Hazel opened her mouth in awe and looked at Callum.

"The man with the magical touch," she said, and then regretted letting that slip. It sounded so sexual.

His eyes heated as he appeared to register the same meaning.

"How did it go today?" Hazel asked, going into the kitchen to resume preparing dinner for herself and Callum.

"Good. Emily Watson is quite the character." He followed her, inspecting what she was doing.

She was making linguine and clams. After that exchange she hoped he didn't guess that she had chosen this recipe because he had said it sounded good.

With everything out and ready to go, she started the gas stove burner and cooked the garlic.

"Is that going to be what I think it's going to be?" he asked, standing close behind her and to her left, looking over her shoulder.

She turned her head, her face inches from his. He smelled like outside and subtle cologne.

"Yes." Her voice sounded sultry to her own ears.

His eyes shifted to hers, then lowered to look at her mouth.

"Are you making that for me?"

"We all have to eat," she said.

He grinned, as if to tell her he knew better.

When the garlic cloves browned, she removed them and dumped them in the sink. They had served their purpose. In their place went three and a half dozen clams, some wine and water. She covered the pan and soon the suite began to smell like the beginnings of a delicious seafood plate.

"Can I help?" he asked.

"Sure. I need a big pan of boiling water."

While he did that, she saw the clams had opened and removed them to cool. She reduced the remaining liquid in the pan, feeling Callum watch her.

"The clams need to be removed from their shells," she said, uncomfortable with the manly way he regarded her, eyes warmer than enjoying the preparation of a good meal would cause. "But leave a few of them in their shells for garnish."

"Roger that." He began removing the clams and she salted the boiling water and added linguine.

"Now what?" he asked.

She put butter into the sauté pan, poured in the clams and added seasoning. Once the ingredients began to boil, she reduced the heat and waited until the pasta was al dente. She strained the pasta and combined it with the sauce. After cooking that awhile, she turned off the heat and tossed in grated Parmigiano-Reggiano.

"Voilà," she said.

He reached past her and picked up a clam.

Hazel swatted his hand. "Contamination."

"I used to do that growing up. Drove the cooks mad."

"It drives me mad. You should have sat through the food safety class I had in college." Spooning the pasta onto two plates, she put the clams in shells on each and then sprinkled a little more Parmigiano-Reggiano on top. She handed Callum a plate and took hers to the table.

Evie had finished her dinner and immersed herself in a coloring book. Hazel and Callum ate in silence for a time.

"This is fantastic," Callum said. "Whoever marries you will have a tough time keeping the pounds off."

Whoever? A quick flash of his being that person

made her pause in taking her next bite. Cooking for him would be fun. Among other things...like sex.

"It promotes exercise," she said.

"Is that how you stay in shape?"

"Mommy takes me on bike rides," Evie said as she colored. "We go camping, too."

"Horseback riding," Hazel said. "I used to hike when I lived in Colorado." Having a child disrupted a routine.

"You like sports?" Callum asked.

"Not softball or football or things like that. Just hiking, biking."

"I want a horse," Evie said with a glance at Callum. "Mommy says I'm not old enough."

"You probably aren't. You could get hurt pretty bad if you fall off."

"I still want a horse."

Hazel had adored horses when she was a kid, too. What wasn't to love? They were beautiful animals. She had gotten Evie some books on horses, along with some model horses that she played with often.

"Well, when you're old enough to take care of it yourself, then we'll talk," Hazel said.

Evie looked at her mother and saw she meant it and didn't argue. She went back to drawing.

"Why didn't you go back to Colorado after you had Evie?" Callum asked Hazel.

She wondered over the suddenness of his question. He must have been thinking about it before Evie had joined the conversation. Was he trying to learn more about her? Was he interested?

"I like it here. I like the community and the climate. It's warmer and drier here. We go back to Pagosa Springs to see my parents, usually on the holidays."

"Don't you want to be closer to your family?" he asked. "Especially with Evie?"

He had hit on one of the things that had kept her away. "Actually, I love my parents but they can be intrusive. My mother would be at my house daily or demand I come see her. She already does that now. She complains she doesn't see us enough. It's like she has a hard time letting us go as kids. We're adults now, with our own lives and aspirations. I wish she'd treat us that way."

"Have you told her that?"

"Yes. She just says she loves me and wants to see me as much as possible. It's better that I'm in Arizona and she's in Colorado, at least for now. I might want to change that as Evie gets older. We'll see. What about you? What kind of relationship do you have with your family?"

"You said you would read to me," Evie interrupted.

"Go get your jammies on," Hazel said.

"Aww," Evie complained, but she went to do as told.

"I'm not very close to them, except Marlowe. I never talked much with my parents. I don't know if that's because my father was so busy working at Colton Oil. I would like to change that, though. Ever since my dad was shot, I've thought about that. I want to be closer to him and the rest of my family."

Hazel thought that was quite sentimental of him. She liked that.

Just then Evie bounded into the room in her pj's.

"Are you ready now?" Callum stood and went to the sofa. Evie grabbed a book from the coffee table and sat right next to him.

Evie's easy acceptance of Callum troubled Hazel. What if she got too attached and then the time to part ways came? Regardless, seeing her daughter bonding with a father figure warmed her and made her yearn to give her that all the time.

She watched as Evie tipped her head to the side to see the pages better and listened to Callum's deep voice reading the children's book. She could feel his affection, hear it in his animated tone. She cleaned the kitchen with a soft smile, not wanting to fall for Callum but afraid she would if he continued to befriend Evie.

Thirty minutes later, Evie's head rested on his shoulder, her eyes closed. Callum put the book on the sofa beside him and carefully lifted the child, cradling her and standing. He looked to Hazel, who led the way to their room. She pulled back the covers and Callum laid her down. Hazel tucked her in.

Then she joined Callum at the foot of the bed. He wore an awed look, no sign of his usual tensing. Evie was working her magic on him. Hazel wasn't sure if just any child could have done that for him. She hoped he would someday get over whatever had happened to make him decide not to protect women and children.

"She's something," Callum said.

"Yes. Of course, she is to me. I'm her mother."

"She seems smart for five. Her understanding of words is really good. Advanced."

His fondness sank into her as she sensed his genuine reaction. He sounded like a proud father. Hazel had noticed Evie was a quick learner, too.

They stood there awhile, until Hazel's awareness of him changed. His feelings for Evie melted her, lowered her guard. An intimate connection grew out of their mutual appreciation of her daughter. Her insides reacted, sparked, and instinct nearly made her move closer. But with him she needed to be careful. She would not make the same mistake she had made with Ed.

She couldn't look away. He lifted his hand and curled it behind her neck. Unprepared for this, she let him lean in and kiss her. His mouth pressed firmly to hers as inexplicable chemistry took over. She put her body against his as she slid her hands up his chest. With that encouragement, he turned the kiss into a flaming ball of passion, pressing harder as they added tongues to the erotic play.

Hazel could barely catch her breath as he devoured her. Callum had his hands on her back, holding her against him. He all but danced her around and guided her through the doorway, into the hallway—and away from Evie—until she came against the wall. Hazel had enough presence of mind to be thankful for that.

Now his hands were free to caress her elsewhere,

and he wasted no time running them over her breasts. She had a crazy thought that making a baby with him would be wild and wonderful. He unbuttoned her blouse. Exposing her bra, he touched her again.

He worked the front clasp and once he had her bared, he stopped kissing her and lowered his head to her left nipple. Next, he lifted her off the floor to bring her more to his level, planting his mouth on her right nipple. Hazel wrapped her legs around him and gripped his head, urging him to her mouth. She wasn't ready to stop kissing him.

Callum pressed his lips to hers and she fell into a whirlwind of torrid desire. She fumbled with his shirt, needing more than anything to have her hands on his chest—a chest she had only been able to look at up until now. Slipping her hands under the material, using the wall for support, she had to draw away to catch her breath.

As she reveled in the hard panel of muscle under smooth skin, Callum kissed her neck and jaw before taking her mouth again.

"Mommy?"

Jarred from this uncontrollable state of sexual frenzy, Hazel jerked her hands from underneath Callum's shirt as he abruptly stepped away and her feet lowered to the floor. He stared at her, visibly stunned but his gaze still lustful.

Appalled by her behavior—just outside the room where Evie slept—Hazel put her clothes back together and rushed into the room, trying to calm her racing heart and breath.

"Yes, honey?"

Evie blinked up at her sleepily, thankfully oblivious to what had occurred in the hall. "Will you turn off the light?"

Seeing the lamp between the two queen beds was on, she bent and turned it off. Then she went to Evie and kissed her forehead. "Go back to sleep, sweetie."

But Evie had already done so, slumbering peacefully. Hazel pulled the blankets up over her tiny shoulders and then returned to the hall, where Callum still stood. He looked much more composed now. In fact, he looked downright aloof.

"Everything okay?" he asked.

"Yes. She just wanted the light off." She studied him carefully. His eyes were a mask now, almost cold they were so remote. He had withdrawn. Granted, that hot encounter had shaken her to her core as well, but he seemed to have withdrawn much more than was warranted. Didn't he marvel over how spectacular it had felt? She did. And she felt slighted that he might reduce it to something meaningless.

"Look... I'm sorry about..." Callum began.

He couldn't even put what happened into words. Maybe he refused to, because doing so would add meaning to it.

"Good night, Callum." Miffed, she went into her room and shut the door, wishing she could slam it. But she didn't want to wake up Evie.

She jerked herself into her pajamas, muttering, "Imbecile," before getting into bed. She turned on the television. It would be a long time before she settled down enough to sleep.

Emily must have given him an earful about her and Evie, in particular about how Ed had run off after discovering Hazel was pregnant. Emily herself had a blended family, having remarried after divorcing her first husband, whom she had met when she was a teenager. No one should ever marry at such a young age. People, at least in Hazel's opinion, needed time to grow before they made such a huge commitment. Spending your entire life with someone was kind of an important decision. Emily strongly opposed a too-impulsive marriage, saying it was just a legality, when love was the thing that kept couples together, not a piece of paper and a few laws.

Whatever Emily had planted in his head, it had made him think. It had brought him closer to Evie, a child and Hazel's daughter, two things he had for some reason sworn off.

Trying to get distracted by the nature program she had turned to a low volume on television, Hazel failed miserably. Her spirits sank when she considered how she'd celebrated the fantastic feeling of kissing Callum, while he apparently shunned such an emotion. The cops had better find that shooter soon. Hazel needed to get away from a man like Callum Colton. She'd be better off with someone more in her league.

Chapter 5

The next afternoon, Callum arranged for a car rental and went to visit a comatose Payne at the hospital. He brought with him Hazel and Evie, who skipped beside Hazel on their way toward the entrance. Callum had noticed a distinct change in Hazel this morning. He wondered if he had mistaken the way she'd said good night and shut the door before he could even respond. Was she upset that he had kissed her? He'd rather have this resolved before going in to see his father. Some of his family would be there and he didn't need to have to explain Hazel's mood.

He stopped her on the cement in front of the doors. "Is something wrong?"

Evie's head tipped up and she looked at him.

"No," Hazel said.

"Last night…"

Evie turned to her mother.

"Don't worry about it. We'll wait for Kerry to find and catch the shooter and then we can both get back to our lives."

Callum met Evie's eyes as she glanced back at him and then she asked her mother, "Mommy, are you mad?"

"Not now, Evie."

Callum could see Hazel was quite upset, her keen gaze firing arrows at him. "I didn't mean to hurt you. It just—"

"Do we have to talk about this now?" Hazel interrupted.

It might not be appropriate to talk in front of Evie, but he doubted she'd really understand and he wasn't going to say anything grossly offensive. "I'm sorry, that's all."

"Yes, I could tell you were."

She thought he was sorry for kissing her? But was he? "Sorry" wasn't the right word. *Concerned* would be a better choice but he couldn't tell her that.

"Don't worry," she repeated, sounding more sincere now. "Whatever you're going through, I get it. I don't need to get involved with another rich guy, so let's just make the best of this situation, okay?"

"Who is Rich?" Evie asked.

Callum almost smiled. Evie thought Rich was a man.

"You're judging me because my family has money?"

"*You* have money. I don't mean to judge. I don't

know you well enough. All I can do right now is go on what I do know."

"My *parents* are rich."

"They don't share any of it with you?" Hazel asked, more of a challenge.

He didn't like what she was implying. "We all have trust funds, but—"

"Well, there you go." Hazel resumed walking toward the door, Evie in tow.

Evie looked back at him and then up at her mother. In the elevator, she asked, "Why are you mad, Mommy?"

"I'm not mad."

Callum watched her as he stood beside her, clearly disagreeing.

Hazel felt a little contrite over her reaction. She couldn't blame him for not feeling what she'd felt in that kiss. Some men treated women poorly, without empathy, and others didn't intend to cause harm. Callum hadn't meant to snub her, humiliate her or make her feel rejected. Even though, absurdly, she had experienced all of those emotions. Or maybe she was just mad for putting herself into a situation that resembled that with Ed far too much.

Callum entered the hospital room first. Hazel was struck by the extent of the medical equipment and the tubes coming from Payne Colton. She had never been this close to someone in such critical condition. She had seen a coma patient on television, of course, but the real thing came with a considerably larger impact.

There were three others in the room, two men and a woman.

"Mommy?" Evie said in a quiet tone, tugging on her sleeve.

"Yes, Evie?" Hazel noticed that everyone except Payne had turned toward Evie, who was oblivious to the attention she'd gained.

"I like Cal-em," Evie said.

"I know you do." Hazel saw a good-looking, dirty-blond-haired man on the other side of Payne's hospital bed smile slightly.

"Don't be mad at him," Evie said, eyebrows arched upward in earnest appeal.

The striking woman with light blond hair looked very businesslike and snickered a bit, while the man next to her in a suit smiled.

"I'm not mad at him," Hazel said, glancing at Callum, whose eyes held a teasingly smug glint.

Evie's expression said she didn't understand. "You were mad."

"Evie, not now," Hazel said sternly.

Evie went into one of her lower-lipped pouts.

"Is my brother stirring up trouble?" the woman asked Evie.

"No," Evie retorted, eliciting a round of laughter.

"How did you manage to make such a fine friend, Callum?" the woman asked.

"Hazel, this is my twin sister, Marlowe," Callum said. "That's her fiancé, Bowie."

"Hello, very nice to meet you. Callum told me

about you," Hazel said to Marlowe. She liked that Callum had such a high regard for his twin.

"And this gentleman over here is Rafe," Callum said, "my younger brother. He's also Detective Wilder's fiancé."

The adopted brother. Hazel recalled Callum telling her that. Not only were the Coltons wealthy, they were all so good-looking! Hotness filled the room. And even though Bowie wasn't a Colton, he was also quite a treat for the eyes.

"I'm going to go get a soda," Bowie said. "Does anyone else want anything?"

"Juice," Evie said.

"A punch or mixed berry is fine," Hazel said.

Everyone else declined and Bowie started for the door. "One juice coming right up," he said.

"How is he today?" Callum gestured toward Payne.

"The same," Rafe said.

They all fell into somber silence.

"What do the police think happened?" Hazel asked.

"He received an email saying Ace was switched at birth and isn't a Colton by blood," Marlowe said. "Naturally, Ace wasn't happy to hear about that."

"The police think Ace tried to kill Payne?" Hazel asked.

"He's the only one who appears to have a motive," Callum said. "But I don't think he did it."

"I don't, either," Rafe said.

"He's our brother," Marlowe said. "Of course he didn't try to kill Dad."

"He said he was home the night of the shooting," Callum said. "There's no video surveillance supporting that."

"Isn't Kerry looking for someone shorter?" Callum said.

"Yes," Marlowe answered.

Callum moved closer to Payne. Hazel watched him take hold of his hand.

"I wish you'd wake up, Dad," he said. "You could tell us yourself who shot you."

Could the shooting have something to do with Ace being switched at birth? Maybe the culprit didn't want to be discovered. Then why send an email making that announcement? Unless the one who had actually swapped the babies wasn't the one who sent the email.

"Do you know who sent the email?" she asked.

"No. I have someone from IT at Colton Oil looking into that," Marlowe said.

"Hey, Callum, how long are you going to be in town?" Rafe asked.

"Indefinitely. I have a new job starting at the end of the month but it is local. I'm free until then."

Marlowe turned her gaze to Hazel, appearing to grow more curious. "When did you two meet? Callum never tells me when he has a new girlfriend."

Why did Callum's twin think Hazel and Callum were together like that?

"Kerry is investigating a murder that Hazel's daughter witnessed," Rafe said. "Callum is protecting them."

"Oh." Marlowe looked from Hazel to her twin. "And you already made her mad?"

"Marlowe…" Callum protested.

"Sorry, brother. I'm not buying it. You look at her like she's more than a client," Marlowe said.

Hazel turned to Callum. He looked at her in a particular way? She hadn't noticed. But then, she hadn't glanced at him much since they entered the hospital room. Every time she did she felt an unwelcome spark, which only brought her back to his regrets over kissing her. She could not afford to want something he would never give.

Later that day, Callum couldn't stop thinking about what Marlowe had said—that he had looked at Hazel in such a way that gave Marlowe the impression they were an item. He hadn't been aware that he had done that. If he had no control over the way he regarded Hazel, wasn't aware of how she affected him, how could he control how he felt about this relationship? Was he calling it a relationship? A zap of alarm pricked him as he realized they were starting to have one. How could he call it anything else? They had kissed. They had almost had sex. They'd have a casual relationship, then.

He walked with her into the inn. They'd go back to their suite and be alone again, except for Evie.

Halfway through the lobby, Hazel stopped, Evie by her side.

"Carolyn?" Hazel asked.

Callum followed her gaze to a woman standing

by a cart full of food chafing dishes. A blonde with a bob in a smart black skirt suit with a white top, she seemed surprised to see Hazel.

He stopped next to Hazel as she leaned in for a hug. Obviously the two knew each other, and judging by the catering supplies, they shared food as an interest. Had Hazel worked with this woman in the past?

"What are you doing here?" Carolyn asked, moving back from the hug, smiling as her eyes roamed over Hazel's face.

"I'm staying here."

"We're being protected," Evie said in her cute voice.

Carolyn crouched down to the girl's level. "Well, hello, Evie. You've grown since the last time I saw you."

"I'm five."

Carolyn laughed a little and stood, sending Hazel a questioning look. "Why are you being protected?" She glanced at Callum.

"It's a long story," Hazel said.

"I saw a man get hit in the head with a rock and he died," Evie said.

Carolyn looked down at her. "Oh, my." Then she returned her attention to Hazel. "Are you all right?"

"Cal-em is protecting us," Evie said.

"That's enough, Evie."

Hazel must say that a lot to her daughter. The more time he spent with them, the more he learned of their close connection. He had always thought a mother and a daughter must have a special bond.

Then his Annabel had died and he'd avoided anything mother-daughter altogether.

"What happened?" Carolyn asked.

Who was this woman and how did Hazel know her? He waited for Hazel to give a quick summary of why they had ended up here and then she finally turned to him.

"Callum is a bodyguard."

"Oh." Carolyn sounded impressed. "A bodyguard, huh? You must be special now."

"Not really." Hazel smiled humbly.

"Yes, she is," Evie said, hanging onto Hazel's arm.

"Callum Colton." He held out his hand to the woman. "And you are...?"

Carolyn's mouth dropped open. "Colton? As in Colton Oil?"

He had grown accustomed to people recognizing him by his surname. They were sort of like celebrities in town; some regarded them in awe and some in loathing, depending on which Colton's path they had crossed. "Payne Colton is my father."

"Oh, yes. I'm so sorry. I heard about your father. My deepest condolences."

What had she heard? "He isn't dead yet."

"But in a coma, right? That's terrible." Carolyn looked from him to Hazel. "How did you manage to meet up with a Colton bodyguard?"

"Completely by accident," Hazel said. "He was across the street when the man was struck and came to help us."

"Aren't you the lucky one?" Carolyn smiled.

"How long have you and Hazel known each other?" Callum asked.

Hazel put her hand to her forehead. "I'm sorry. How rude of me. Callum, this is Carolyn Johnson. She owns Carolyn's Kitchen. I told you about working for her."

"Yes, I remember. Very nice to meet you."

After a moment where she seemed miffed that her friend hadn't mentioned her, Carolyn looked at Hazel. "She was one of the best chefs I've ever had."

Callum thought she sounded wry, even cynical, and wondered why.

"Thank you, Carolyn. You always treated me so well. Restaurants can be so stressful, but you were always calm and courteous."

Hazel didn't seem to notice her friend's tone. Pleasing customers with food did seem demanding, as did the work hours. Service jobs were unfortunately thankless, most of the time. A shame, given how enjoyable going out for dinner or whatnot was.

"We have to keep customers coming back." Carolyn sounded faintly derisive.

Hazel looked at the cart behind her. "You're making a catering delivery? You normally have others do that."

"Yes, normally."

Hazel hesitated, finally registering Carolyn's sarcasm. "How are you doing? H-how's the restaurant?"

"Oh, I had to close it."

That came as a total shock to Hazel, Callum saw

by her rounded eyes and dropped jaw. "No. What happened? You were doing so well."

"Yes. After you left, I couldn't find another chef as good as you. And me?" She lifted her eyes and glanced at Callum ruefully. "I am not a cook. I'm a businesswoman. This lady, however..." She gestured toward Hazel. "She is *amazing.*"

She sounded different now, not so brash. Did she mean the compliment?

"Carolyn. I'm so sorry. I had no idea. You should have called me." Hazel seemed genuinely remorseful, as though she felt responsible for the closure.

"You made your decision and you gave me more than enough notice." Carolyn shrugged. "The luck of the draw, I guess. The chefs I hired after you left couldn't prepare the meals the way you did. Customers slowly stopped coming. And then I had a bad review and it was all over. I got out before it ruined me completely. Now I work for a catering company." She gestured back at the cart. "A tough transition, going from entrepreneur to servant."

Callum was good at reading people and he could tell her transition had been especially difficult. Carolyn made a good show of being a good sport but the loss had to be painful. Who wouldn't feel that way after accomplishing so much, just to lose it? He felt bad for her. He couldn't imagine how Hazel felt.

"Is there anything I can do to help?" Hazel asked.

"No. Don't worry about me. It's been really great to see you again. How is your food delivery service going?"

Hazel paused before saying, "It's going all right. I wouldn't say I'm a raging success. I'm staying afloat."

Carolyn smiled. "I'm sure it's just a matter of time before you are a raging success, artist that you are. I know firsthand how your cooking can make a big impact on revenue."

"Oh, my gosh, Carolyn. I never intended to cause you to lose business. I set everything up so the recipes would be easy to follow. You shouldn't have suffered at all."

Carolyn shrugged again. "You made quite an impression for me, you know."

Hazel seemed confused. "No, I didn't know that."

"I don't see how. Patrons asked to thank you personally all the time. They complimented your cooking to me more times than you know. I didn't tell you at the time, but I was very worried about how things would go after you left. I respected your decision, though, and didn't want to influence you. You were my friend more than you were my chef."

"Oh." Hazel leaned in and hugged Carolyn again. "I wish you would have told me. I could have worked part-time for you or something. Anything to help you not lose your restaurant. I know how much it meant to you."

Moving back, Hazel looked at Carolyn with heartfelt sympathy and regret.

Carolyn met the emotion with stiffening aloofness. She didn't like pity, that much Callum could see. Neither did he.

"Really, Hazel. I'm a grown woman. I can take care of myself. I'll do the servant thing for a while and then start up a new venture. You know me. I'm no quitter."

Callum believed that. He didn't really know the other woman but she had an indomitable energy about her. No wonder she and Hazel were such good friends. While Hazel wasn't aggressive, she had tenacity and ambition as well as talent.

"No, you are not. And you are a smart businesswoman. You belong in your own element."

"Ms. Johnson?" a voice interrupted.

Callum saw a hotel worker approach Carolyn.

"We're ready for you," the hotel worker said.

Carolyn turned to Hazel. "Have to go now. So nice running into you."

"You, too." Hazel touched her arm before Carolyn pushed the cart, following the hotel worker, probably to a conference room.

It took Hazel a few long seconds to start walking toward the elevator with Callum. She apparently had fallen into melancholic thought.

"Why do people always think it's their fault when decisions they make result in others having a run of bad luck?" he asked.

That pulled her out of her reverie. "W-what?"

"You aren't responsible for other people's misfortunes."

They stepped into the elevator, Evie holding Hazel's hand, head tipped back as usual. Her curiosity made her listen intently to everything said by the adults around her.

"I created the recipes," Hazel said.

"Which should have helped her."

"It did, but you heard her. The chefs she hired after me couldn't replicate them."

He took a moment to marvel that she didn't see what he did. "You're an artist first, Hazel."

She blinked a few times as though startled by what he brought to light.

"Your passion went into every one of those recipes, those meals you oversaw in the kitchen," he said.

"But…they had the recipes and I wrote detailed instructions."

"*But* they didn't have the heart. Only you had that. You made Carolyn's Kitchen."

"No. Carolyn made Carolyn's Kitchen," Hazel argued. "She was an aggressive businesswoman. Driven. Smart. She hired me to help her make her dream a reality. She was a good person."

"Then she should have gone to culinary school if she wanted to run a restaurant," he said.

Hazel rubbed her forehead with two fingers.

The elevator doors opened and Evie tugged Hazel toward the exit. Callum wanted to say more, do more about this discussion. But he walked to their suite, mindful of the energetic Evie, and let them inside.

Evie bounded toward the television and Hazel set her up with an animated show. Then Hazel walked into the kitchen—and took out a pizza from the freezer. No gourmet meal for tonight.

Glad Evie's overactive mind had something to keep her occupied, Callum joined Hazel behind the island, where Hazel had picked up a pen and hovered the point over a notepad.

He wasn't fooled. She used idle tasks to help ease her tormented thoughts.

Putting his hands on her upper arms, he asked, "Did you leave on bad terms?"

She shook her head. "I gave her a lot of notice."

"Then why are you beating yourself up over this?"

She put down the pen and ran her hand over the top of her hair. Facing the living room where Evie watched television, she stilled. Callum didn't think she registered Evie's presence all that much, so absorbed did she appear to be in her separation with Carolyn.

Finally, she turned to him. "I left for selfish reasons. I had Evie and…"

"You had to look out for your own."

"Yes, but Carolyn would have never betrayed me."

Callum moved to stand near her, gripping her shoulders and making her face him. "It's okay to want to forge your own way in life. You don't have to work hard to make others succeed. I think, deep down, you knew you had greater potential than what you got working for your friend."

Hazel's captivating, green-gold eyes met his soulfully, and she added a slow and telling shake of her head. He had nailed what she felt.

"Am I right?" he asked to make her confront it.

With teary eyes she nodded.

He drew her into an embrace. "You followed your heart, Hazel. No one can condemn you for that, least of all me. I did the same."

His father hadn't been happy with his decision not to join the Colton Oil team. Neither had his mother. "I know what it's like to want something others don't understand or expect from you."

"I just hate to see good people fail," Hazel said.

"I bet she'll have a comeback. Maybe she won't open another restaurant but she'll find success somewhere."

At last the first glimmer of a smile emerged on her pretty face. She had her hair back today, exposing her expressive eyes, prominent cheekbones and full lips he longed to kiss right then.

"That's better. A woman like you should never be sad," he said.

Her smile expanded. "Why me?"

Why indeed? He had to think a minute as to why he'd even said such a thing. Although he inwardly cringed with the truth, he said, "You're beautiful inside and out."

"Wow, the last man who said something that nice to me probably lied."

He was glad she made light of such a serious compliment. "Ed?"

"Yes. He said sweet nothings to me a lot. He had me really believing I was special."

Wait a second. Was she making light or did she think Callum had just said something nice and was being insincere about it?

"Surely you've had others. I can't be the only one who complimented you over the last five-plus years."

"No." She shook her head and moved into the kitchen. "No one."

He followed her, leaning against the island counter as she began to prepare dinner. "No one?" There had to have been *someone*.

"No one serious," she said.

But she had dated. "How many have you dated?"

She made a funny face. "You make it sound like I slept with all of them."

"Unintended. How many guys have you been out with?" He discovered he really wanted to know.

"Not many. Three. No, four. Two were one date and the other relationships lasted a few weeks."

He reflected on his own experiences. Annabel had died almost five years ago. He and Hazel had been single and getting past old hurts for the same length of time. Maybe for too long. Hazel had a better excuse than he did. She had Evie to keep her busy, and it would be a lot harder for her to find a man suitable to take over a father role.

Father role.

"What about you?"

Hazel's question spared him from painful memories. He had already faced more of those than he could deal with.

"Girlfriends?" Had she capitalized on the direction of their conversation?

"How many have you *had* since your last serious

relationship?" She grinned before opening the oven to check on the pizza.

Wily woman. Lucky for her, this was something he could talk about.

"Not many. Seven."

She planted her hands on the counter beside him. "Seven?"

That was a lot to her? "Yes. Minimal dates."

She mouthed *minimal dates* and scrunched up her brow in question. "You cannot tell me that some of those women didn't mean something more than a date."

As she chopped lettuce for what he presumed would be a healthy salad to go with their not-so-healthy pizza, he realized she had concluded he had had not more than a casual fling in the past five years. How could she? She knew nothing about him, really.

"What happened to you?"

Her earnest question put him at odds with how to respond. "Nothing."

She chopped a carrot, the knife hitting the cutting board hard. "Did any of them matter?"

"They all mattered."

She continued chopping and, without looking at him, said, "No. Really matter."

He had to be honest. "They all mattered, Hazel. They just deserved better than what I could give."

"How many were you serious with?"

Why did she ask? Why was that important to her? Was she trying to find out what she was up against?

"Five or six. Some lasted a few months, others a week or two. One pretty recent." When it got too serious, then he walked.

She stopped chopping the poor carrot, her head bowing slightly and her shoulders slumping equally indiscriminately. Still keeping the knife on the cutting board, flush with a carrot, she turned her head to see him. "What happened, Callum?"

He silently cursed. No one had ever pushed him like this. He glanced over at Evie, who was still engrossed in her movie and not paying them any attention.

He had never told anyone about Annabel. Few knew she had been his girlfriend. Back then, he had been mainly in Texas, but he worked a lot. He had drifted away from his family, only seeing them on Christmas and Thanksgiving. He had brought Annabel to both holidays that last year. When asked later if he was still seeing her, he had only said no. Now he was about to tell Hazel. Why her?

He met her eyes and could feel his soul pouring out through his. She blinked solemnly, putting down the knife and facing him. She put her hand on his cheek. "It's okay. You don't have to tell me."

The selflessness of her saying that tore through all of his resistance. She meant it. She respected his sensitivities. The connection between them strengthened, his to her, anyway. She was someone he could trust. Maybe it was timing more than anything else. Maybe, finally, he was ready to put in words what he had so far kept to himself.

"She died nearly five years ago." Saying that felt like a regurgitation, it came up from inside him like sour milk. He felt sick. He put both hands on the kitchen island counter and lowered his head. "I've never told anyone this."

Hazel's hand touched his back, high and on the left. She caressed him in comfort. She didn't press him, just waited. He could go on or he could stop right there. She wouldn't force anything out of him.

"She was pregnant." Callum choked back a powerful wave of anguish.

"Oh," she breathed in heartfelt empathy. Not pity, no sympathy, just a profound understanding. She was a mother. She must know how terrible it would be to lose her child.

"We knew it was going to be a girl," he said, barely getting the words out before his anguish became too unbearable.

Unable to continue, he pushed off the counter and walked toward his room.

Chapter 6

Hazel ordered room service the next morning. She had picked at her dinner the night before while Evie devoured hers. Callum had not come out of his room the rest of the night. Hazel had lost her appetite after hearing his gut-wrenching confession. She could not imagine the awfulness of losing a person you loved and a child all in one fell swoop. She had to assume he had really cared for the woman. Such crushing emotion would not have overcome him had he not.

She prepared Evie's breakfast of cereal and fruit. Evie had complained about the fruit but Hazel said that after junking it up last night, she had to eat healthy today.

Hazel sat down at the dining table and began eating with her daughter. Looking at Evie's inno-

cent face as she scooped milky bites into her mouth,
Hazel thought again about how difficult it must be
for Callum to be around them. She had thought
about that a lot since the previous night. She also
had so many questions she would never be able to
ask, would not ask. How had the woman died? How
long were they together? Were they engaged? Did
he love her as much as he appeared to? Now she understood why he usually refused to take cases involving families.

He had broken down just voicing that she had died
and their unborn baby girl along with her. Callum
was not a weak man mentally. He was tough, fear-
less. Look at his profession. He was a bodyguard,
one of the best in the world. But talking about the
woman from his past had brought him to his knees.

And then there were the other thoughts she had.
The selfish ones, like, what did his loss mean for her,
Hazel? She could no longer deny she had begun to
have feelings for him. What would it do to her if he
decided to turn away? He had already withdrawn
and it had been nearly five years since the tragedy.
Five years. Something terrible must have happened.
Something sudden. A car accident? No one ever got
over losing love—or a child.

"Mommy?"

Grateful to be pulled out of her never-ending con-
templations, she looked at Evie.

"You're not eating."

Hazel hadn't touched her cereal. She still wasn't
hungry. "I know."

"How come?" Evie swung her legs under the chair and table.

"I have a lot on my mind."

"Cal-em?"

"Finish eating, Evie." Dang if her daughter wasn't a perceptive little thing.

"Were you mad at him again?"

"No."

"Good, because I want him to be my daddy."

Where had that come from? Daddy?

"He's not your daddy, Evie."

"But I want him to be. I want a daddy. Everybody else has one. Why can't I?"

"Someday you might." Hazel couldn't predict when and she wouldn't rush into anything. The man she married would have to prove himself a good person and role model for Evie.

Callum could be.

Hearing Callum enter the room, Hazel hoped Evie would stop asking all her questions and expressing that she wanted a father.

"Good morning," Hazel said.

Callum was all cleaned up and ready for the day in jeans and a long-sleeved white button-up. Sexy as hell. He didn't seem reluctant to see her after what he'd told her. He seemed back to his normal self—and guarded again.

"Good morning." He picked up the box of cereal Hazel had left out and poured some into a bowl she had also had ready for him. Then he sat across from Evie, who sent him a big smile.

"Somebody got plenty of sleep last night," he said to her, smiling back.

Evie giggled as she chewed a mouthful of cereal.

Callum reached over and put his hand over Hazel's, catching her by surprise. She met his sobering eyes.

"I'm sorry for leaving you the way I did last night," he said. "I've never told anyone about Annabel."

Hazel sensed she had a chance to ask questions. She'd be careful not to push him. "Not even your family?"

He shook his head. "They knew I was seeing her, but they don't know she died."

Her heart went out to him. He had suffered for so long in silence. "Callum, why?"

Pulling his hand away, he looked down at the bowl of cereal. "I…couldn't."

Until now, with her. He had told her.

"Were you engaged?" Hazel asked.

"Not yet. I was going to propose the next weekend."

Seeing him drift off into that dark place, Hazel refrained from asking how the woman and the baby had died. This time she put her hand on his. "Thank you for telling me, Callum. I know how difficult that was for you." He looked at her, the darkness fading. "I want you to know if you ever need someone to just listen, I can be that person for you."

He took her hand in his. "I know you can, but I'm not sure I'll ever be able to talk about her again."

After long seconds of staring into his candid eyes, Hazel nodded. "Okay."

"Are you going to be my daddy?" Evie blurted out.

"Evie," Hazel admonished. "That is rude." Clearly she hadn't understood anything Hazel and Callum had just said. Adult talk.

Callum chuckled. "What makes you ask that, Evie?" Callum asked.

"You keep touching my mommy."

"Your mother is a very good friend of mine."

"I would like you to be my daddy," Evie said.

"Evie, that is enough."

Callum chuckled again and Hazel realized he had done so because she repeated "that's enough" to Evie a lot. She smiled at him and then Evie.

The suite phone rang and Hazel went to answer it.

"Ms. Hart?"

"Yes?"

"We have a package that was delivered by courier for you at the front desk."

That was odd. She hadn't forwarded her mail, but was having it held at the post office. She'd pick it up there on occasion.

"All right. Could you have someone bring it up?" She hung up and faced Callum, who looked at her in question.

"There's a package for me at the front desk."

He immediately looked concerned.

Moments later a hotel worker knocked on the

door. Callum answered, taking a cardboard overnight delivery envelope.

Well, it couldn't be a bomb. It was too thin, and looked like it contained a letter.

He inspected it and then ripped open the top, taking out a typed letter. After he read it, he handed it to her.

In capital letters it said:

I WOULDN'T GET TOO COMFORTABLE IF I WERE YOU. JUST BECAUSE YOU'RE WITH A COLTON NOW DOESN'T MEAN YOU'RE INVULNERABLE.

She looked up at him. "The shooter knows we're here." This was a small town and the Dales Inn the only hotel, but being stalked like this scared her.

Nowhere she and Evie went would be safe. The shooter would find them. Hazel looked at her daughter, who had moved into the living room and was watching a cartoon. If anything happened to her...

Hazel recalled how devastated Callum had looked when he told her his baby girl had died with her mother. Hazel wouldn't survive losing Evie.

He took out his phone. "Hello, Kerry. Someone sent Hazel a threatening letter." When he disconnected he said to Hazel, "She's on her way."

Hazel looked at her daughter again, imagining the shooter hitting her over the head with a rock or shooting her little body. She dropped the letter and put her hand to her mouth.

Callum came to her and pulled her into his arms. "I won't let anything happen to her."

"We can't stay in this inn forever."

"You won't have to. Kerry will find him."

"In the meantime, what if he gets to us? He seemed certain."

He rubbed her back. "I won't let him hurt you. He'll have to get past me to get to you and I won't let that happen."

She believed him, but even with his expertise, he couldn't be one hundred percent sure. She leaned back and met his eyes. Pressed this close to him, with his arms still around her, and especially with their deepened connection, her sexual reaction to him was stronger than ever before. His eyes grew darker with passion. He had to feel the same.

If Evie hadn't been in the room, she would have kissed him. Last night and this morning, Hazel had been tempted to take a chance on him. She had never met a man since Ed who made her feel they could have something lasting.

Easing away, she took a seat at the kitchen island. Callum bent to pick up the letter and placed it on the counter. They waited a few minutes and Kerry called Callum to say she was on her way up. Moments later, he let her into the room.

"Hey, Evie. I've got something for you." Evie turned from the television as Kerry went to her and handed her a MVPD baseball hat.

Evie inspected it and then put it on her head with a giant smile.

"What do you say, Evie?" Hazel said.

"Thank you!"

Kerry straightened and walked over to the island, where Callum handed her the letter.

She read it and frowned.

Callum gave her the envelope, handling it lightly to preserve fingerprints—if there were any.

"I'll run some forensics on this but my guess is whoever typed this was careful not to leave any traces," Kerry said. "I will check security and can track down where the envelope was mailed from and maybe find out something that way. It might take me some time, though."

"Whatever you can do," Callum said.

The next few days were anticlimactic in that no one sent any more threats and they saw no suspicious characters in the few people who visited their suite. Callum decided it was time for a surprise to break up the monotony—and provide some relief from the constant awareness of Hazel and how much he would like to stop fighting to keep things professional.

A sudden knock on the door signaled the arrival of the surprise.

Hazel looked up from her work in the kitchen, preparing another week's worth of food deliveries while wearing a sexy blue flowing sundress and no shoes. He loved a barefoot chef. He held back a smile as he went to the door to let Patsy Cornwall inside. The assistant led a hotel bellboy into the suite. The bellboy pushed a cart that held a big box and some bags of other items.

"Something for a young girl," he said.

As soon as Evie spotted the packages, she squealed and charged to the entry. The box contained a finished dollhouse mansion. The bags contained everything to furnish it.

He put the box in the living room and let Evie go through all the accessories.

"You didn't."

Glancing up, he saw Hazel had left the kitchen to get a closer look. "I did."

"Callum, this is too much."

"No, it's not. We're cooped up in here. We'll all get a kick out of this." The dollhouse had turrets, curving staircases going up three levels and two porches. The miniature house had incredible detail, from the exterior Victorian trim to interior wallpaper and paint. Evie was going to have a blast.

Callum sent Hazel a mischievous glance.

She looked at her daughter, who was ecstatic over the plethora of doll items.

"You're going to spoil her."

He wanted to spoil her. After seeing her play with her Barbie and how her imagination soon soared, he knew he had to get her one. He had asked Patsy to get every piece of furniture she could find and to include the little things, like dishes. Patsy had it overnighted from a store willing to work with them in a hurry. He had requested it a few days ago. She might break a few things at her age but she'd have this for years, maybe even into adulthood.

It took him a while to set up the dollhouse. Evie had all the accessories scattered on the floor behind the house, which she'd already begun to fill with furniture.

This is what it would have been like with his daughter, had she lived. Callum pushed those thoughts away and went around to the back of the house to help Evie arrange the rooms.

She let him take over and began dressing two Barbie dolls.

"This is Angie," Evie said, showing him the doll dressed in a sparkly dress.

"She's pretty, like you."

Evie beamed up at him before going back to her dolls. He finished arranging furniture and got out of her way.

She instantly dove into playtime, speaking in a low voice, pretending the dolls were talking about going to their new house.

He left her to it and went to the kitchen, where Hazel was cleaning up after a day of cooking. "What's for dinner?"

"Spaghetti."

"Nothing too fancy. Too bad." He dipped his finger into the sauce for a taste.

She swatted the top of his hand. "Raised the way you must have been, you didn't spend much time in a kitchen."

They'd had servants to do the cooking and serving. "Your cooking is irresistible." He could get accustomed to this, a delicious meal every day…and a beautiful woman by his side.

That thought came unbidden. She *was* a beautiful woman, no denying that. And he could get accustomed to a delicious meal every day. What troubled him was much more than how those two things appealed to him. The idea of living with them made him feel good. Too good.

"Why don't you set the table?" Hazel asked.

Callum did so, enjoying the sense of being part of a family unit. Hazel put food on the table and had to force Evie away from the dollhouse. They all sat together, something he hadn't often done with his family growing up. The Coltons had formal gatherings and sat together on holidays. He and his siblings had tremendous respect and love for one another, but Callum had drifted apart from them after Annabel passed. Since he'd been back in town, he had grown closer to Marlowe and Bowie. And he couldn't imagine Ace could ever have shot their father…

He ate dinner without talking, because he feared he could not survive the cost to his heart. Despite all his efforts to steer clear of women with children, he was falling headfirst into a powerfully moving relationship with Hazel and Evie. Where had all his resolve gone?

Hazel tucked Evie in to the sound of Callum cleaning the kitchen. She hadn't missed his joy in seeing Evie's excitement over receiving the extravagant gift. Sharing dinner tonight had been especially poignant. He genuinely adored Evie. He looked at her as though they had been a family for years. When he let his guard down—unaware or not—he was a phenomenal man. Evie could look up to someone like him.

That terrified Hazel.

She had to know more about him before they sank into a lovestruck quicksand.

"I'd like a glass of wine before we turn in," she said. "You?"

A few seconds passed before he said a tentative, "Sure."

After she had two glasses on the counter, she took out a chardonnay from the cooler and found an opener. Manly hands took over from behind her. Putting her hands on the counter, she watched him open the bottle, feeling his arms on each side of her.

After he uncaged her with one arm, she rolled to lean on her lower back against the counter.

He handed her a glass.

Taking it, she said, "Princesses all over the world must have cast a spell on you."

"I've protected many princesses."

His deep, chocolaty voice and intimate tone riveted her. "You have? Like who?"

"They were from Morocco, Spain, Japan and Sweden. Most of them are repeat clients and usually need me when they travel."

Which must be often. He lived such a glamorous life. He came from a wealthy and prominent family and he protected affluent people. But then, he must be used to that way of life.

He was so different from the kind of man she had envisioned for herself after Ed ran off. She couldn't forget the promise she had made. Up until Ed, she had left her fate to chance, believing that everything happened for a reason and that the right man would come along naturally. Well, Ed had come along naturally, all right, but he'd turned out to be all wrong. Nothing should be left to chance. Maybe some things happened for a reason, but finding a good man was not one of them.

After sipping some wine, she asked, "What made you decide to become a bodyguard?"

He took a moment before he answered. "I was on a mission in Ukraine and noticed two men waiting outside of an apartment building. A young woman came out and they abducted her. I followed them. Watched them force her out of the vehicle and into a house. They had her blindfolded and tied."

Hazel listened with increasing horror.

"I went to the door and knocked. One of them answered and I gave him a throat strike." He gestured with his hand, putting his fingers to her throat. "I heard the girl screaming down the hall and the other man yelling for her to shut up. I heard him hit her and tell her he'd kill her if she didn't be quiet. By then I was at the doorway. He had already torn her shirt and was trying to remove her jeans. He saw me and stopped and asked who the hell I was. I told him I would be the last person he'd ever see alive if he didn't get off the girl." He stopped as though back in the scene.

"What happened?" she asked.

"He got off her and lunged for his gun. I threw it out of reach and gave him a good beating. Just before I knocked him unconscious, I told him if he ever hurt another woman again I'd come back and finish him off." He drank some wine.

"Then what?"

"I called the police and told them what happened. The two were arrested and sent to prison."

"What happened with the girl?" Had she been the woman he had lost?

He shrugged. "She thanked me and I never saw her again. That was my last mission before my service ended and I left the navy."

Callum had done a very heroic thing and that woman had to have been so grateful. If that had happened to Hazel, she would have wanted to find the man who saved her from rape and possibly murder, to thank him when she wasn't traumatized.

Looking at him and his handsome face and messy hair and into his blue eyes, she fell for him even more. Although she tried to ward the feeling off, the warmth mushroomed and gave her a tickle in her stomach.

"When I returned to the States, I didn't know what I wanted to do with the rest of my life. All I knew was I didn't want to work at a corporation, especially Colton Oil."

Hazel hadn't expected him to continue talking, but welcomed it.

"Being a SEAL taught me how to fight and use guns and do both really well. That was my skill set. I ran into an old friend who told me about Executive Protection and put me in touch with the CEO."

"And the rest, as they say, is history," she said, admiring his tall, muscular frame and his SEAL background that he put to good use. She sipped wine and put down her glass on the kitchen counter.

"A little more history than I like," he said.

Could it be he'd talk about the woman he had lost?

"I almost stopped working for Executive Protection a year after I joined."

"Because of her?" she asked quietly.

He nodded, the mood turning darker. Putting his glass beside hers, he walked into the living room and stopped before the windows.

Hazel followed, standing beside him and resting her hand on his forearm, urging him to face her.

He did.

"Tell me, Callum." It would help him if he talked about it. And since she was losing her fight not to fall madly in love with him, her best interest was to help him help himself.

"I was protecting a witness in the trial of a drug dealer who murdered someone," he said. "I did my job and saw that the witness made it to court, testified and sent the dealer to prison." He stopped.

Hazel could see he had come to the most difficult part. She stepped closer and put her hands on his im-

"One Minute" Survey

You get **TWO books** <u>and</u> TWO Mystery Gifts...

ABSOLUTELY FREE!

YOU pick your books – WE pay for everything!

See inside for details.

YOU pick your books –
WE pay for everything.
You get TWO new books and TWO Mystery Gifts...
absolutely FREE!
Total retail value: Over $20!

Dear Reader,

Your opinions are important to us. So if you'll participate in our fast and free "One Minute" Survey, **YOU** can pick two wonderful books that **WE** pay for!

As a leading publisher of women's fiction, we'd love to hear from you. That's why we promise to reward you for completing our survey.

IMPORTANT: Please complete the survey and return it. We'll send your Free Books and Free Mystery Gifts right away. **And we pay for shipping and handling too!**

Thank you again for participating in our *← We pay for* "One Minute" Survey. It really takes just a minute *EVERYTHING* (or less) to complete the survey... and your free books and gifts will be well worth it!

Sincerely,

Pam Powers

Pam Powers
for Reader Service

"One Minute" Survey

GET YOUR FREE BOOKS AND FREE GIFTS!

✓ Complete this Survey   ✓ Return this survey

1 Do you try to find time to read every day?
☐ YES   ☐ NO

2 Do you prefer stories with suspenseful storylines?
☐ YES   ☐ NO

3 Do you enjoy having books delivered to your home?
☐ YES   ☐ NO

4 Do you share your favorite books with friends?
☐ YES   ☐ NO

YES! I have completed the above "One Minute" Survey. Please send me my Two Free Books and Two Free Mystery Gifts (worth over $20 retail). I understand that I am under no obligation to buy anything, as explained on the back of this card.

240/340 HDL GNPS

FIRST NAME	LAST NAME

ADDRESS

APT.#	CITY

STATE/PROV.	ZIP/POSTAL CODE

READER SERVICE—Here's how it works:

◄ If offer card is missing write to: Reader Service, P.O. Box 1341, Buffalo, NY 14240-8531 or visit www.ReaderService.com ◄

BUSINESS REPLY MAIL
FIRST-CLASS MAIL   PERMIT NO. 717   BUFFALO, NY

POSTAGE WILL BE PAID BY ADDRESSEE

READER SERVICE
PO BOX 1341
BUFFALO NY 14240-8571

NO POSTAGE
NECESSARY
IF MAILED
IN THE
UNITED STATES

pressive chest, encouraging him without words. The painful storm in his eyes eased a little.

"No one knew he wasn't just any dealer. He was high level and dangerous, with ties to one of Mexico's most notorious cartels. Living in the shadows of the underworld. I was seeing Annabel during the trial. She lived in the city where we met. The dealer must have found out. She was run off the road and killed."

Hazel felt his pain, shared it and wished she could take it away.

"I protected the witness but I couldn't protect Annabel or our unborn child," he said, grinding out the words with deep and barely leashed anger.

"Listen to me, Callum." Hazel had to reach him now. He was vulnerable. "You didn't know he would send someone to kill her. It is not your fault."

"The person who ran her off the road was never found. I tried, but…"

Hazel touched both sides of his face. "You didn't kill her. The drug dealer did."

"He did it to get even with me. To make me pay."

"It is not your fault." She stopped him from turning away. "I know people say that too much, but it's true, Callum. An evil man killed her, not you."

"I vowed to never protect women and children after that."

Hazel slid her hands to his shoulders. "But you protected princesses."

"That was different."

"How?" She watched him ponder that. Princesses were women. Some of them had to have kids.

"I don't know. They didn't make me think about Annabel."

She had a question she dreaded to ask because she was pretty sure she'd hate the answer. "Do I make you think about Annabel?"

"You make me have to try very hard *not* to. You and Evie both."

Well, that was better than an all-out yes. "You need to confront your grief, Callum. Have you talked with Annabel's family?"

"Not since the funeral."

"Maybe you should. It might give you closure."

"They blame me."

"That's what they said? Are you sure they really blame you? Any parent would be distraught over losing their child. Have they tried to contact you?"

"They invited me to a gathering they planned on the one-year anniversary of her death, but I didn't go. Even if I'd wanted to, I was out of the country. I didn't get the invitation until after the memorial."

"Do they know about the baby?" she asked.

"Yes. Annabel told them."

"And no one in your family knew you went to her funeral?"

He shook his head. "At the time all I thought about was getting away."

He had submerged himself in work, traveling all over the world, never taking a break to be with family or friends. What a lonely existence. And the burden he had carried with him must have been suffocating at times. Hazel couldn't believe he hadn't told anyone about the baby. Well, maybe she could. He hadn't been able to talk about them.

Until now. With her.

Hazel became aware of his hands on her hips. At some point during their exchange he'd placed them there. Her body pressed against his. Her gaze melded with his, seeing into him without barriers. He'd opened himself to her and their connection blossomed.

"Why me?" she asked, her voice low with rising desire.

"I wish I knew." He lowered his head and kissed her. His lips touched hers, featherlight, brushing over them and then taking her mouth for an intimate mating.

After he had poured out his heart to her, Hazel felt secure in giving herself to him. Everything.

Chapter 7

Hazel looked up at Callum when he broke from another impassioned kiss. His eyes burned with lust, fueled by the significance of what he had confided, as though freed. She reveled in the deep meaning in his next kiss, and was glad she had put Evie to bed. She had the night with Callum. With his arms around her back, she looped hers over his shoulders.

He lifted her and she wrapped her legs around him as he carried her to his room, kissing all the way to the bed.

Hazel had to fight for a few seconds of clarity before this continued.

"Callum, I'm not on the Pill."

He rose above her, looking intently into her eyes.

She didn't want him to stop but they had to behave like adults.

"I don't have anything, either. I have something at home but I didn't bring it."

Neither one of them had thought they'd end up in the same bed, especially this soon. She did some quick calculations.

"I just had my period. We should be safe."

She spent a long moment wavering between temptation and logic. He had to be thinking the same thing. What if she got pregnant? How would she feel about that? Was this worth the risk?

Her heart charged forward with an affirmative while her brain cautioned to slow this down. Lying here like this, with him hovering over her and her hands on his hard chest and the vision of his face, so manly and full of desire, temptation hummed into a roar. She could feel his member against her. Kissing had made her hot; this wasn't lessening the effect.

"Are you sure?"

He wasn't asking if she was sure about the timing. He asked if she was sure if she wanted to take this risk.

"Are you?"

He lowered his mouth to hers for a soft kiss. "I asked you first."

"I'm sure." Especially now that he had resumed kissing her.

"Me, too." He kissed her harder, lowering his body onto hers and sending lightning bolts of sensation through her.

She sank her fingers into his thick hair and moaned. In response to that sound, he moved against her, teasing, hinting at what would come.

Sliding her hands down to his T-shirt, she lifted the hem. He moved back and removed the shirt the rest of the way, sending it sailing to the floor while his eyes devoured the sight of her. The blue sundress dipped modestly low in the front, but there was enough cleavage to show off.

He lifted the dress up and she sat up as he pulled it over her head and dropped it on top of his shirt. His eyes took their fill of her naked breasts before he came down and sampled one in his mouth, flicking the nipple while his hand ran over the other breast.

Eager to see him, she tugged at his jeans' button. He withdrew and helped her, having to get up to take them off. Convenient that they were both already barefoot. She kicked off her underwear and waited for him to climb back on top of her. She was traditional that way. She loved the feel of a man's weight on her before he entered. While that was her favorite position, it most certainly wasn't the only one she enjoyed.

Callum crawled over her and slowly lowered his body onto hers. A delicious shiver coursed through her. He kissed her softly for endless moments before kneeing her legs apart. She was ready to give herself to him, more ready than she had been for any man in a long time.

He guided himself to her and slowly pushed into her, filling her deliciously. The initial friction against her sensitive spot drove her to near orgasm.

"Wait. Wait," she rasped.

He stilled above her, his breathing faster and his eyes ablaze.

Hazel dug her head into the pillow against unbearable pleasure. She didn't want her first orgasm to end so quickly. But he turned her on so incredibly much!

Callum groaned. "I can barely hold still when you look so sexy and beautiful." He withdrew and thrust into her and then repeated the action over and over, moving her body on the bed and sending tingles of ecstasy radiating from her abdomen all the way out to her limbs.

She bit back a cry as she came on an explosion of orgasmic fireworks. He groaned again and slowed as he experienced his own release.

Then he put his head beside hers, each of them catching their breath.

"That was incredible," he said next to her ear.

"Like the Kentucky Derby, except the most exciting two minutes in sex."

He chuckled, then rolled off her to prop his head on his hand. "Are you usually this responsive?"

"No. Ed had to work at it for at least fifteen." Suddenly disturbed by that revelation, Hazel averted her eyes from Callum. What was different about Callum?

After a moment, she turned her head and saw his thoughts had taken a sober turn as well. Not wanting this moment or the beauty of what had just transpired to fade yet, she rolled onto her side with her back to him.

"We can at least spoon for a while, can't we?" she asked.

After a few brief seconds, he moved closer and said above her ear, "Yes."

The feel of him against her calmed her and enveloped her in warmth. When his hand caressed her arm and he planted a soft kiss on her cheek, she knew he had fallen under the same spell, the spell that had landed them in bed together. Tomorrow would bring whatever it brought.

Callum ordered room service the next morning. Hazel had gotten up after him and gone into her room before Evie woke. Now Evie was busy with her dollhouse and Hazel was finishing getting ready. He'd heard her shower turn off a few minutes ago.

When he had first awakened to Hazel's sleeping face on the same pillow as his, he had been overcome with affection and arousal. Her ankle was over his calf. Her plump breasts were molded into tempting mounds above the sheet and blanket. He could start every morning like that.

And that was precisely the thought that had sent him careening back to reality. Annabel's face rushed forth. He didn't feel guilty or that he had betrayed her. It had been too long since she had died. It was more of a threatening feeling. He was in danger of welcoming a woman and her five-year-old girl into his life. He had failed at protecting the last mother and daughter he had been involved with. Did he want to take that risk? No. At least not now. He didn't know if he'd ever be ready for that.

Hazel's responsiveness to him had only increased

his pleasure and, if he were brutally honest, the bond he felt with her. It was too overwhelming. Too potent.

He had told her what he had told *no one*, not a living soul other than Annabel's family. He recalled the day of her funeral, when her father had asked why no one from his family had attended. He had said they couldn't make it. Annabel's father had looked at him strangely. He didn't know it at the time, but all Callum had wanted was to leave and be as far away from any reminders of Annabel as he could.

Annabel's murder had occurred in another city, not Mustang Valley. Another police force and even the feds had investigated but with no real zest. It had been assumed her killer had fled to Mexico. It hadn't made big news. No one in his family or circle of friends had heard about it, by some miracle. He had needed to be left alone.

No one would have understood. No one who hadn't gone through what he had would be able to understand. The terribleness of her murder. The helplessness of not being able to find her killer. The knowledge that her murder and the killing of their unborn child would never be solved.

There wasn't a day that passed when he didn't think about that. Who was her killer and where was he today? Did anyone know what he had done and could it lead police to him? Was there a way to extradite him to the States if he was abroad?

Maybe that was what he needed. Annabel's cold case solved. Maybe then he could move on. Maybe then he wouldn't think about what was taken from him so violently whenever he spent time around women with children. Pregnant women got to him the most. He had missed out on that.

One could argue he could find another woman and start a family, but for him it wasn't that simple. Not only had Annabel and their unborn baby been taken from him, so had all of the first-time experiences and the happiness. The wonder of the creation of life, the stages of pregnancy, the anticipation of the birth. Looking up names. Imagining being a family—a *close* family.

Everything good about being with a woman who was pregnant with his child had been destroyed. All that came to his mind now in connection with pregnant women was Annabel's lifeless and abused form on the coroner's table, the baby bump still there, but full of death now.

He had put up with enough when it came to family, so why did he have to go through that? His was not an idyllic family. His former stepmother, Selina, loved drama and enjoyed driving wedges between his siblings. Callum never understood why his father allowed her to keep her job at Colton Oil. Everyone thought she must have something on Payne. She also kept jovially reminding everyone of the Colton Oil bylaws that said the CEO had to be a Colton by blood. With the discovery that Ace was switched at birth, that presented a significant problem. Her heartless pokes reminded Callum of his estrangement from his father and how terrible it would be if Payne never woke up from his coma.

He snapped back to the present and poured Evie some cereal. "Evie, come get breakfast."

Saying that made him feel like a father figure. Taking care of Evie came so naturally. How had that happened? Would he ever be the same after this?

Just then Hazel appeared in jeans that hugged her slender hips and a silky white top. She eyed him peculiarly and he knew she wondered why he'd gotten out of bed before she woke. Was she gauging him? Maybe she hoped he was an early riser. More likely she thought he had run away.

He put the room service on the table. "Coffee?"

"Sure."

He felt her continue to evaluate him as he finished getting their breakfast spread out on the table.

"I'd like to talk with Kerry about what we can do to help with the investigation." He watched her ascertain why he was so anxious to help. Or maybe she wondered why he'd so abruptly made that announcement. He needed something to do and he needed to get away from her as fast as possible.

"Okay," she said slowly. She sat and sipped the coffee he'd poured.

He sat across from her. Evie bounded to the table and took her seat, oblivious to the tension between her mother and Callum. She scooped up her cereal and looked toward the television.

"What did you have in mind on the investigation?" Hazel asked.

"Nate Blurge was the murder victim Evie saw

being kidnapped. Maybe we can find out more about him."

She nodded a couple of times. "Okay."

"Did you know him or of him at all?"

"No. I never went to bars like Joe's."

Of course, she wouldn't. Not only did she have a young child, she wasn't the kind of woman who would frequent places like that. Maybe he had asked just for something to say that wasn't related to last night.

"You were up early," Hazel said.

"Yeah. I couldn't go back to sleep."

"Something troubling you?" She took another sip, doing a poor job of appearing nonchalant.

"No." He ate his breakfast, hoping she'd just let it drop.

Turned out, she did, but she was way too quiet as they left the inn to go to the police station.

Outside, he gave the valet his ticket.

Evie clung to Hazel, trying to swing off her mother's arm.

His rental arrived and he opened the back door for Hazel to get Evie in her car seat. Then he opened the front passenger side and went around to get behind the wheel. She was still quiet as they headed out, but only for five minutes.

"Did you love her?" Hazel asked.

He had often thought of that. He hadn't known Annabel long before she had become pregnant, but as time passed and the birth of their child drew nearer, he'd thought he could love her. They never had the passion he and Hazel shared last night. That confused him.

"I have to believe I did, yes."

"Do you still?"

That stopped him for a few seconds. He hadn't really contemplated that since she died. Now as he reflected on it, he realized he did not.

"No," he finally said.

"Then…why?"

She was reading too much into him getting up before her. He got it that she was suspicious, but why grill him like this?

"I just woke up before you, Hazel. Did you want me to wake you?"

She didn't answer right away and he let her take her time in contemplating what he'd said.

"I wouldn't have been with you had I thought you'd turn me away the next day," she said at last.

Where had that notion come from? "I didn't turn you away." Was she the cuddling type? He used to be.

Evie's father must have really done a number on her. Was Callum another mistake to her?

"You seem different this morning," she said.

"I don't mean to be." He wished she wouldn't push the issue.

"Are you okay with us?"

He glanced in the rearview mirror and saw Evie fast asleep in her car seat. No wonder Hazel was talking so freely. Now he had to answer, and he hesitated because he had to be honest.

"I take it by your silence that you aren't. I'm sorry

for making such a big issue about it, but I need to be sure about how to handle this going forward."

He heard sincerity in her voice. She didn't like asking all these questions. She just felt she had to. "Everything is going so fast between us. I haven't had time to process it. Have you?"

She breathed a laugh of relief. "No. We can slow it down. Is that what you want? I have Evie to think about. She's already so fond of you. I worry about her when it comes time to part ways—if that happens."

"I don't ever want to hurt Evie, so I'll do whatever you think is best when it comes to her."

"What about me? Will you do what you think is best when it comes to me?" She said it lightly, but he sensed she actually needed to know.

"It isn't my intention to hurt you. I'm trying to be honest with you."

"I appreciate that, but I'm a little disappointed in myself for not thinking this through better. We rushed into this and now I wish I hadn't."

They had rushed into sleeping together. Could they have done anything to prevent their attraction? He couldn't blame her for being regretful or concerned. They barely knew each other. About the only things they did know were a little background information and that they had a hot physical chemistry that was apparently uncontrollable.

"I don't regret last night at all," he said. "In fact, that's what has me in such a conundrum today. I have never had such an amazing time, except maybe my first time."

She averted her head, propping her elbow on the door frame and curling her fingers against her chin. "That has me in a conundrum, too."

Her quiet, soft tone revealed her vulnerability. He reached over and covered her hand with his. "We'll cool this off for a while. Get to know each other more."

She looked at him as though having serious doubts as to whether either one of them could cool this off.

Suddenly, the glass of Callum's window shattered as a bullet flew past him and went through the passenger window. An instant later, he realized someone had shot at them, narrowly missing him and Hazel. "Get down!" he shouted, looking in the back at Evie, who had slouched enough in her sleep to be below the door frame but now began to wake.

As he took out his pistol, his heart pounded as he urgently searched for the shooter. An SUV had fallen back in the other lane but sped up as Callum had done the moment the bullet had penetrated.

He weaved in and out of traffic, putting more distance between them and the shooter.

"Call 911," Callum said to Hazel, who had already taken out her phone.

He slowed enough to make the next turn, trying not to frighten Evie more than she already was. She had begun to cry. Cars ahead blocked his way. This wasn't a movie—he couldn't drive up onto the sidewalk.

Hazel finished talking to the dispatcher.

The gunman began to gain on them. Callum's fear that Evie would be harmed intensified.

"Callum." Hazel sounded terrified. "Evie."

"I know."

He tried to veer out into the oncoming traffic to get around a car. He had to steer back into the lane. The car passed and Callum would have tried again but the gunman was beside them in a big black SUV. The shooter aimed. Callum pressed on the brakes. The other man did too and then rammed into them.

"Evie, stay down!" Hazel hollered, dropping the phone.

"Mommy?"

"Just stay down."

Callum didn't want to shoot unless he had to, not with a child in the truck. The traffic began to clear. He drove into the oncoming lane and gunned the truck, passing two cars before getting back over as another vehicle approached, horn honking. With some clear road, Callum raced toward the police station, unable to believe they were being chased again, that he had allowed it to happen.

If he hadn't been distracted by Hazel and their night together, he could have stayed focused and prevented this—at the very least putting Evie in less danger.

He made the last turn to reach the station. In the rearview mirror he saw the SUV pass without turning. The gunman knew they were headed for the police. He also must know the police would come after him if he tried to wait for them again.

"He's gone," Callum said.

Hazel breathed heavily and put her head back.

He drove into the police station parking lot and parked.

Hazel jumped out and hastily removed Evie from the car seat. When she had her daughter in her arms she asked, "Are you all right?"

"I'm fine, Mommy. Did we almost have an accident?"

"Yes, sweetie. Mommy just had a big scare."

Callum put his hand on her back as she scanned the area. "Let's get inside."

They walked inside. Kerry would be expecting them. Callum had phoned ahead. A few minutes later, she appeared, sporting her badge on her belt.

"How are you doing?" Kerry asked.

"We were chased again and shot at," Hazel said, putting Evie down.

"Where is he? I'll get some cars out there."

"It's too late. He didn't follow us all the way to the station," Callum said.

"I'll have them be on the lookout for the vehicle."

Hazel gave her the plate number, surprising Callum with her stealthy observation and thinking. She went on to describe the SUV, including the damage to the passenger side when the shooter had rammed into them.

"What brought you here today? Not drawing the shooter out and trying to run you down?"

"We'd like to help with the investigation. Speed it up if we can."

Kerry looked from Hazel to Callum and then Evie. "We've questioned some of the workers at

Joe's Bar. Nothing very concrete has come up. We did learn that Nate Blurge's wife works there and he had a reputation for flirting with a lot of women, many of them the waitresses there. Apparently he made a lot of husbands angry. If the killer was one of them, he might show up. If you could watch the place, see if you can find out anything about who might want him dead. If you help out with that, I can pay more attention to his family."

Callum nodded. "We can do that, but not with Evie."

Hazel shook her head. "No, not with Evie."

"Is there anywhere you can take her?" Callum asked. "Didn't you say you had a brother who was a cop in Phoenix?"

"I did. His wife is a cop, too."

"That sounds about as perfect as it gets," Kerry said. "I agree. Evie is in too much danger if you keep her here. Every time you leave the inn you're at risk. Whoever is after you is watching that place very close."

"I hate the idea of parting company with my daughter but I can't argue she's in danger. She'd be safe with my brother and his wife."

Callum liked that idea. Not only would it keep him from bonding even more with the girl, he wouldn't have to worry about protecting her *and* her mother.

"Why don't you go back to the inn?" Kerry said. "I can have an officer escort you."

"That won't be necessary," Callum said.

"Are you sure? It's too dangerous for you to come

and go from the inn and I'm concerned next time you won't get away without being harmed."

Or killed. Although she didn't say so, Callum knew she worried they could very well be murdered.

"I'm sure." He would not let his guard down again.

"We need to come up with a way to get you out of the inn and Evie somewhere safe." She tapped her lower lip with her forefinger and then lowered her hand. "How about if I have someone drop off some disguises so you can get Evie out safely? Then I can arrange for undercover officers to watch you and make sure you get on your way."

Callum grinned. "I like that idea. In fact, I know the perfect disguises." He leaned close to Kerry's ear and told her in a low voice what to get for them.

Kerry smiled and glanced at Hazel.

"What are you up to?" Hazel asked Callum.

"You'll see." Then to Kerry, he said, "Just ask Patsy to pick them up. She'll have fun with that."

He gave Kerry Patsy's contact information, looking forward to the trip to Hazel's brother. All that time they would spend together as a family… And then he would be alone with Hazel after they dropped Evie off. That came with so many conflicting emotions. Leaving Evie would be sad, but being alone with Hazel gave him all kinds of unwelcome thoughts…and welcome ones, too.

Chapter 8

Later the next morning, Hazel couldn't believe what she had allowed Callum to talk her into wearing. She looked at herself in the mirror. The studded leather sleeveless top zipped up to just above her breasts and the low-hipped leather pants hugged her shape. The jewel encrusted shoes with four-inch heels would bring her much closer to Callum's height. A blond wig completed the ensemble.

Beside her Evie giggled. She had a wig, too, also blond, and wore an adorable biker girl T-shirt with leather pants—not skintight like her mother's. Patsy had also gotten her a fun metal rivet and leather wrap bracelet and a pair of black boots.

Evie posed in front of the bathroom mirror, only her head above the sink counter.

Hazel chuckled. "Come on, Evie."

They left the bathroom. Callum waited for them in the kitchen, leaning against the island counter, holding his phone. His eyes lifted as they approached, frozen in that pose as his gaze roamed down Hazel and then back up.

"I'm a biker girl!" Evie jumped and stopped in front of him.

"You sure are. Looking good, too."

"Hopefully you haven't ruined her future," Hazel said with humor, enjoying this and feeling like they were a family getting ready to go on an outing. She wouldn't even analyze that right now.

She did have a moment where she had to stare at him, though. Dark blue jeans that cupped his crotch and a leather jacket over a gray T-shirt that had a black print on the front. He also had on glasses to ramp him up from lowly biker to biker with money. She liked his wig, black with a tasteful ponytail.

"Are we ready?" he asked.

"Yeah!" Evie called out cheerily.

"Let me check outside first. I have my rental car waiting in front of the inn," he said.

He had prepared well for this. And even though her disguise was a bit sexy, all of them were convincing. They looked completely different than they had this morning.

In the lobby, Hazel took Evie's hand, and Callum noticed a man walking with another woman staring at her.

She looked away, stopping before following Callum through the doors. He covertly checked the front of the inn and beyond and then turned, still holding the door open, not saying he'd spotted a dark SUV across the street. The driver turned their way, stared a few seconds then turned away. A man and a woman with a child wasn't unusual. They might stand out as a biker family but they looked nothing like they usually did. Callum was pleased the man apparently hadn't caught on to their disguises.

Hazel stepped outside with Evie. The car was right in front of them, a valet having already opened the back door.

Ushering Evie into the seat, Callum let Hazel bend to buckle her in. She looked through the opposite window at an SUV. The driver still wasn't even paying attention to them. Callum saw he wore a cap and sunglasses, so recognizing him was still impossible. Callum thought it might be the same man who'd come after them before.

He saw another man ogling her as she got in the front passenger seat. Callum got behind the wheel, looking over at the SUV. The driver glanced their way but didn't seem to have any peculiar reaction.

"This costume is attracting too much attention," she said.

"Good, nobody is going to guess it's you."

"Evie might have made that SUV driver suspicious," she said.

"Evie won't be with us after today."

As they moved out of the inn's parking area, Callum glanced once more at the SUV. The driver paid them no attention as they passed. Evie would be safe. Callum leaned back, savoring the victory. He didn't understand why or how, but Hazel and Evie were so important to him. His job of protecting them was so important to him. He looked over at Hazel, gorgeous and content in their successful getaway. He'd seen her satisfied in another way, too, and struggled to ward off the temptation to see that again.

"Hazel?"

Hazel's brother was a couple of inches over six feet and built like a linebacker. Off duty, he sported jeans and a Kansas City Chiefs T-shirt. Callum could see the resemblance to Hazel in his thick dark hair and hazel-green eyes.

"Is that you?" her brother asked.

Hazel smiled big. She had called ahead to make sure Owen could take in Evie but she must look so different than her usual self right now. "Yes."

"And Evie?"

Evie giggled. "Yes."

"What's with the look?" Her brother opened the door wider to let them in.

"I'll explain." Hazel entered the house.

After a two hour drive they'd arrived in this neat and tidy suburb of modern homes, some stucco, some more traditional, all with big front windows. Hazel's brother's house was two stories with a covered porch and a three-car garage.

The grayish-brown wooden floor of the foyer

opened to a formal living room, with the kitchen and dining areas to the left. Stairs led up to the second level beyond the dining room.

"Callum, this is Owen and Jessica, my brother and his wife." Hazel introduced them.

Callum shook Owen's hand as his wife walked up beside him, a stunning woman with long dark hair and brown eyes. They made a handsome couple.

"Hi," Jessica said with a wide, toothy smile.

"Hey there, Evie." Owen crouched to Evie's level, who clung to her mother's leg in a sudden show of shyness.

"You remember your uncle, Evie," Hazel said. "Say hello."

"Hi," Evie said quietly.

Hazel laughed, her affection and adoration coming out in the sound.

Callum hadn't thought Evie had a shy bone in her body but meeting new people apparently made her withdraw. She'd done the same to him when they had first met. Kids.

"You've grown since I last saw you," Owen said.

A beagle came trotting up with a wagging tail.

"Do you remember Olive?" Jessica asked.

"Yes." Evie crept out from behind Hazel's leg and knelt down before the beagle.

Eager for attention, the dog jumped up on her, paws on her legs. Evie giggled and collapsed onto her rear. When she crawled on hands and knees into the living room, Callum knew she'd be preoccupied for a while.

"We were surprised you were coming up today," Owen said. "Such spontaneity isn't like you. We were glad we're both off duty today. Is everything all right?"

"There's a good reason for us showing up on such short notice, and looking like this," Hazel said. "Evie saw a man get hit on the head with a rock and his body was found."

Jessica inhaled sharply. "Oh, no. She saw that?" She glanced back at Evie as though wondering if she was okay.

"Evie seems fine," Hazel said. "She seems unaffected."

"She's probably too young to fully understand what happened," Callum said. "The problem is the police haven't caught the killer yet, and he knows where we're staying."

"He's tried more than once to get us."

Owen kept an unreadable but somber face but Jessica's jaw fell.

"Evie?" Jessica asked, incredulous.

Hazel nodded. "That's why we're here." She looked at her brother. "I need a huge favor."

"You want us to watch Evie? You don't even have to ask," he said. "Of course we'll do it."

"And she'll be safe," Jessica said. "We're both armed and have licenses to carry."

"She'll be guarded at all times," Owen said.

Callum saw Hazel's shoulders slump in relief. "I can't thank you enough," she said. "You don't know how much it means to me to know she'll be with two cops. I won't have to worry about her the way I have been."

"Of course," Owen said. "We'll love having her." He glanced over at Evie and Olive, who were rolling around the living room in play. "And so will Olive, it would seem."

Hazel laughed and Callum smiled a little at the cute sight of Evie and the dog.

"Do the police have any solid leads?" Jessica asked.

"We're looking into the murder victim right now. Hopefully that will point us to a suspect," Callum said.

"Where are you staying?" Owen asked. "Is there security?"

"Callum is a bodyguard." She explained how they met and how Callum had saved her and Evie. "He's kindly agreed to protect me until the killer is caught."

"Bodyguard, huh?" Owen said, checking Callum out. "Do you work for a security service?"

"I work for Executive Protection Services. It's an international personal protection agency."

Owen's brow lifted and he seemed impressed. "Sounds flashy."

"He's protected princesses," Hazel said. "Not your everyday bodyguard."

The way she looked at him snared his attention. He doubted she meant to reveal her admiration so guilelessly.

"So it would seem," Owen said.

"We were just about to have lunch," Jessica said. "Are you hungry?"

Callum wasn't but Hazel glanced at Evie and said, "Evie hasn't eaten yet."

"I hope chili cheese dogs are okay." Jessica led the way into the open, bright kitchen.

"*Yaaay*, hot dogs!" Evie bounded into the kitchen and took a seat at the table, Olive right by her side, sitting on the floor beside the chair.

Jessica prepared some paper plates, serving Evie first and then the men at the kitchen island.

Hazel sat at the table with Jessica.

Callum wasn't very hungry so he knifed off one bite and set down his utensils.

"So, a bodyguard, huh?" Owen asked, picking at his food.

"Yes."

"What's your story? How'd you get into that profession?"

"I was a Navy SEAL before that and the opportunity presented itself when I left."

"SEAL. Not many can make it through that training," Jessica said, sounding impressed.

"No." No point in denying it. SEAL training was beyond extreme.

"What made you decide to be a SEAL?" This question came from Hazel.

He hadn't thought about that in a really long time. Growing up he hadn't always aspired to be a SEAL. "I was an aggressive kid. Always getting into fights. Staying out late and getting in trouble. I was never arrested, just kind of...wild. My last year in high school I wondered what I wanted to do with my life. Not follow my father. A friend of mine suggested the military. He had a good point. If I continued on my path of aggression, maybe I would have ended up in jail. When I was a kid, I would play with toy soldiers. The army didn't appeal to me but the navy did. The SEALs always fascinated me. The challenge of becoming one satisfied my headstrong nature. So I tried out and made the team."

"You were wild?" Hazel asked. "You're so level-headed now. So calm."

"I thank the discipline of training for that. It changed my life." The years he had been active had been enough. When he left, he was ready for something different. Being a SEAL had served its purpose. He had learned how to channel his aggression, put it to good use. Being a bodyguard continued to do that for him. He felt fortunate to have found his true calling in life. Not many people did. He would have been a lost soul if he had chosen to work an office job.

"You said you were staying somewhere together?" Owen asked.

"At the Dales Inn," Hazel said.

"You're staying with my sister?" Owen asked Callum.

"For her protection. And Evie's, up until now."

Owen glanced from him to Hazel and back again. "Are you sure there isn't another reason?"

Was he being a protective older brother?

"Owen," Hazel said in a cautionary tone.

"Are you seeing him?"

"What difference does that make?" she asked.

"So you are?" Owen looked at Callum.

"No. We aren't *seeing* each other. He's helping me, that's all." But Hazel averted her head, a dead giveaway that she wasn't being completely truthful.

"Hazel has been through a lot," Owen said to Callum. "Did she tell you about Ed?"

"She did."

"So you understand she needs a man she can depend on."

"Owen, stop." Jessica laughed a little. "He's always been protective of Hazel. Don't mind him. I'm sure you're a decent guy and wouldn't hurt her."

"I wasn't there for her when Ed left her. That won't happen again." Owen said the last directly to Hazel.

"Everything is all right, Owen," Hazel said. "I'm not doing anything I don't want and I won't do anything that will hurt me or Evie." She turned to Callum. "Especially Evie."

Callum put his hands up. "I am a decent guy and I would never harm Hazel or Evie." He looked at Hazel. "Not intentionally."

He couldn't promise she wouldn't end up with hurt feelings after this was over. He couldn't predict the future, much less their chemistry. That had a mind of its own.

"All I ask is you don't tell anyone Evie is staying here."

"We would never put her in that kind of danger," Owen said, Jessica shaking her head in full agreement.

They finished eating and now it was time to go. Callum saw how difficult this was going to be for Hazel. She watched Evie play with Olive with somber eyes.

"She'll be fine," Jessica said. "We have toys for my nieces and nephews, my siblings' kids, so she'll have plenty to do."

Hazel sent her a grateful but bittersweet smile. "I've never been away from her like this before."

Jessica put her hand on Hazel's shoulder. "You'll see her again before you know it."

Hazel nodded, wiping her eye even though no tears had fallen. She did look a little misty, though. She went to Evie and crouched.

"Hey, Evie. Mommy's going to go now. I'll be back to get you as soon as I can, okay?"

"Okay." Evie stood and turned to hug her mother, not seeming at all afraid to stay with her aunt and uncle—and their cute beagle.

Hazel kissed her head. "You be good for Aunt Jessica and Uncle Owen, okay?"

"Okay." Evie plopped back down by Olive, whose tail wagged and head moved forward for a quick lick on Evie's face.

Evie giggled and petted the dog.

Hazel stood and walked to the entry where Callum waited. She glanced back once more before saying goodbye to her brother and Jessica.

Just then, Evie bounded over, throwing her arms around one of Callum's legs. "Bye, Cal-em."

Callum knelt before her and she hugged him around his neck. "Bye, Evie. We'll see you soon."

"'Kay." With that, she ran back to the dog.

"How long did you say you two have been living together?" Owen asked incredulously.

"Not long. A week or so," Hazel said.

"You must be good with kids," Jessica said.

"Maybe so. Evie is a good girl," Callum said, seeing Hazel wasn't amused. She was probably concerned over how Evie would react if he left them.

Callum couldn't do anything about how much Evie liked him. He could be careful with her, though—and Hazel.

They left the house.

Outside, Hazel rubbed under her nose as though the sting of tears threatened her composure. "Is she even going to miss me?"

Callum chuckled. "She'll have a lot of new things to keep her preoccupied. But yes, she'll miss you and she'll be so excited to see you again."

Hazel smiled slightly. "And you, it would seem."

"I'll be mindful of that, Hazel."

"She's already so attached to you."

"She likes me. I haven't been around her long enough to make that big of an impact. It will be the same as saying goodbye to a friend at school."

"It *will*?"

He hadn't meant to sound as though he had already decided to part ways with her when this was over.

"If this doesn't end up turning into something more," he said.

She glanced at him with appreciation for the clarification. As they reached the car, Callum wondered why he had reassured her. The prospect of their becoming a real couple—maybe even a family—gave him a sick feeling. He would never forget the way he had felt when Annabel died, along with their unborn baby. His soul had been ripped from him. He hadn't been able to function. He had wondered if he would ever make it through.

No more talk about the future for him and Hazel. He'd make sure she was safe and then that would be that.

Since they were already dressed in disguise, Callum suggested they start staking out Joe's Bar. Nate Blurge was known to have spent a lot of time there, as Kerry had said. Someone had to know something that might lead to a break in the case. Hazel stepped into the dimly lit bar with Callum. Right away her first impression was that the lights were low to conceal the disrepair. A melting pot of people half-filled the place with its dirty, worn floor, and scratched and chipped tables and chairs. The ceiling had water stains and dirt caked the twenty-plus year old trim.

"Have a seat anywhere," the bartender called out.

No Wait to Be Seated sign here.

Two young couples laughed at a table. Solitary patrons at the bar watched the television that hung above shelves of liquor or stared at their drinks. A group of scary-looking biker men loitered around a pool table. The tallest one zeroed in on Hazel, making no effort to hide his ogling.

Callum chose a table in the middle of the bar. Hazel sat adjacent to him. Moments later a scantily clad waitress approached with a name tag that said Shelly. Callum ordered a beer and Hazel ordered a chardonnay.

"Hey, isn't this the place where that man who was murdered hung out?" Callum asked.

Hazel was amazed at how quickly he went to work.

"Nate?" the waitress replied. "Yeah. He was here most nights. Been kind of peaceful without him."

"Oh, really? Why is that?" Callum asked.

"He liked to flirt with all of us girls. Nate wasn't the handsomest man you ever saw. Shame he was killed and all, but I didn't know him very well. I'll be back with your drinks." She left for the bar.

Hazel watched her get their drinks from the bartender and walk back over to them.

"Did Nate sleep with any of the waitresses?" Callum asked.

Shelly slowed as she placed the glass of wine in front of Hazel. "Why do you want to know?"

Callum shrugged dismissively. "Maybe that has something to do with why he was murdered."

"Police already came in asking questions." She set a bottle of beer in front of Callum.

"Did they talk to anyone who had relations with him?"

"Don't know for sure. He bragged to me once that he had a thing going with Candace."

"Candace?"

"Yeah. She works two jobs. Has a day job in town."

"Is she here now?" Hazel asked.

"She only works weekends here," Shelly said.

"Did he engage with anyone else?" Callum asked.

"I didn't keep track of his love interests. He mostly annoyed me and the other girls."

Kerry hadn't mentioned anyone named Candace. Could it be they had stumbled upon something?

The waitress left to visit other tables.

Hazel looked around the bar, at the bikers who gave her an uneasy feeling, at the cheerful pair of couples and the line of solitary men at the bar. She was about to turn back to Callum when she noticed one of the men at the bar was staring at the waitress who had just served them.

The waitress turned from a table and the man quickly averted his head. As she passed behind him, he looked at her again and watched as she retrieved more drinks from the bartender and then walked to the table of couples.

"What is it?" Callum glanced behind him and saw the man. He followed his gaze and also where Hazel looked.

"That man," she said. "He's watching that waitress."

The waitress returned to the bar, going behind it. She smiled at the man who had been staring at her and they began to converse.

"They seem to know each other," Callum said.

The man at the bar reached over and touched the woman's hand and she smiled differently now, much more warmly. Then she glanced at the bartender as though making sure she hadn't been seen. The man seemed to respect that and pretended to pay attention to his bottle of beer.

"The ghost of Nate Blurge?" Hazel said.

Callum chuckled. "Yes. He might be flirting vicariously through that guy." If the woman Blurge had flirted with was the killer's wife, maybe that was why Nate was murdered. And maybe the new man who flirted with her would draw the killer out.

"I have to go to the bathroom." She stood and made her way to the back corner, having to pass the group of bikers on the way.

She ignored the tall biker, aware that he followed her movement. She finished her business in the bathroom, washed her hands and left.

As she walked past the pool table, the tall biker stepped in her path. She stopped.

He wore a sleazy grin, or at least that's how she interpreted it.

"Hey, how about a game of pool? You can invite your friend over." He gestured toward Callum. "Is he your boyfriend?"

She contemplated lying. "No."

"Oh." His gaze roamed down her body and back up again. "What's your name, pretty lady?"

"Excuse me." She moved to go around him but he blocked her way.

"If not tonight, then maybe another night?" He gestured toward Callum again. "Maybe when he isn't around?"

"No, thanks."

"At least tell me your name. Can I have your number? I think we should get to know each other."

"Look, I'm not interested." Hazel stepped aside.

The tall biker took hold of her arm and she got a whiff of his breath. He had been drinking for some time.

"Let go of my arm." She jerked her arm and he held firm.

"Tell me your name."

Just then Callum's hand flattened on the man's chest. "What do you think you're doing?"

"Hey." The tall biker stumbled back with Callum's shove. "I was just talking to the lady. She said you and her weren't a couple."

"She also told you she wasn't interested. Is there a problem?"

The tall biker shook his head, feigning nonchalance and acting as though he wasn't afraid. "No problem."

"It looked like you weren't letting the lady pass."

"I would have let her pass. What business is it of yours anyway?" The man stepped forward, as though trying to intimidate Callum.

Callum stood at least an inch or two taller than the biker. "She's with me. And even if she wasn't, I can tell when a woman doesn't want to talk to a man and she doesn't want anything to do with you."

"You don't know that. And you don't own her."

"Come on, Callum." Hazel put her hand on his forearm. "Let's go."

"You gonna hide behind a woman now?" The tall biker stepped even closer. "You should have stayed out of this. If you hadn't shown up, I'd have her number by now."

"She wouldn't have given you her number."

"Well aren't you a cocky bastard. Maybe somebody needs to put you in your place."

"Maybe you should quit drinking and go home. I don't want any trouble. I was a Navy SEAL, so you should think twice about starting something with me."

Callum didn't brag. He sounded calm and as though he had given the man a courteous warning.

But the tall biker smirked and glanced back at his cohorts. "Did you hear that? This jerk is a SEAL. He thinks he's better than all of us."

"I'll warn you once more. You don't want to start anything with me."

Hazel backed up a little. This could get ugly. She had no doubt whatsoever that Callum could take on all of the bikers. Maybe if they were sober the other men would have had a chance, but all of them looked inebriated.

Two of the bikers stepped forward, one holding a pool cue.

"You don't look like you ride. You're too pretty," the tall biker said. "What makes you think you can come in here and get between me and a lady?"

"She doesn't want to talk to you," Callum said.

"I'm getting tired of you saying that." The tall biker took a swing, which Callum easily avoided. He ducked another attempt and then delivered a hard uppercut to the jaw.

The tall biker stumbled backward and the one with a pool cue tried to jab Callum.

Callum blocked that and outmaneuvered him for control of the stick. He swung the cue, knocked the third man on the head and then kicked the taller one, sending him flying back onto the pool table.

This was turning into a real bar fight. And Callum could really move. She almost wasn't afraid, she was so in awe of him.

Hazel backed up some more when the biker who had come after Callum with the cue charged. Using the stick, Callum blocked his punching fists and twisted to high-kick his face. When he landed he used the cue to poke the second man and then tossed it aside to hit the taller biker twice. His opponent fell down.

The other two backed off. Hazel noticed everyone in the bar had stopped to watch, even the bartender. Fighting must be the norm here, because no one interfered.

Callum waited for the taller man to decide what to do. He stared at Callum as he got to his feet, wiping blood off his lip.

"Come on, man. Let's play pool," said a biker who hadn't joined the fight.

The taller biker looked from Hazel to Callum and

then finally swatted the air with his hand. "She ain't worth it." With that he faced his friends.

Callum turned and found Hazel, putting his hand on her lower back.

She walked with him toward the exit, Callum tossing money on their table on the way out.

"That was quite a spectacle back there," she said when they were outside.

"They were drunk."

"Clearly. You could have seriously hurt them."

"Yes. I'm glad he chose not to engage anymore."

"Did you learn all those moves in the navy?"

"I refined them in the navy. I got into bar fights a lot when I was young."

"Right. Wild." She smiled and laughed a little, trying not to be so turned on by him.

Nobody had ever fought for her, least of all at a bar. She had not been the type of girl who hung out at such establishments, especially like this one. She had always been more of a wine bar kind of woman. Lunches with her girlfriends. Dates to nice restaurants.

Walking beside Callum, covertly taking in his long strides and his big shoulders, slightly swaying, she had never felt safer.

He caught her looking at him. "What?"

She shook her head, fumbling with brief self-consciousness. "Chivalry isn't dead."

"You liked it that I got into a fight back there?" He grinned teasingly. "I wasn't playing around."

"Oh, I know you weren't." She eyed him again, unable to stop her admiration.

At the car, he stopped her before she opened the door. "Maybe I should get into fights more often."

She tipped her head up, falling into this flirtation far too easily.

"And you in this outfit doesn't help matters." He touched beneath her chin. "I've been dying to do this all day."

He kissed her, soft and slow. Then the flames took over and he deepened the caress. He didn't touch his tongue to hers, just gave her a long and reverent kiss.

She was beginning to think avoiding another tumble in bed would be impossible. And as for avoiding falling for Callum? That was becoming even more impossible by the moment.

Chapter 9

Back at the Dales Inn, Callum saw that same SUV out front with someone inside. Funny, now that he had a closer look, this man didn't appear as large as the one who had shot at them. He must have been mistaken about the suggestion that this was their shooter.

"We should be fine. Just don't look at him." If it was a man. Callum wondered if it could be a female.

Up in the suite, he called Kerry, who told him she was on her way to check on them.

"Is there anyone else you can think of who has a grudge against you?" he asked Hazel.

Her head popped up from the tablet she had been playing around with. "What?"

He went over and sat beside her. "It just occurred

to me that the person who's been sitting out in front of this inn might be a woman."

Her brow scrunched in confusion. "But the person who almost ran me and Evie over was a man. I know it."

"I know that, too."

"Well…what are you suggesting?"

"Maybe nothing. I'm more thinking out loud." He ran his fingers through his hair. "I just have this feeling that there is someone else seeking you out. The person who sits outside the inn doesn't shoot at us."

"We were in disguise."

Yes, but every time? What if Callum hadn't noticed the driver of the SUV before today?

"Can you think of anyone who might have a reason to be angry with you?" he asked.

She frowned in confusion. "Callum, I don't understand why you're asking me that. You think there is someone else—besides the kidnapper Evie witnessed—who is after me?"

"Yes, and no. Like I said, I'm thinking out loud, making sure I cover every angle."

After a moment she slowly shook her head. "No."

She seemed hesitant.

"What about your ex-boss? Carolyn Johnson?" The woman had lost everything after Hazel left her restaurant. People murdered for different reasons and revenge was one of them. Not that he could say for certain that Carolyn would try to kill Hazel. Maybe she stewed over her losses and blamed Hazel, but hadn't gone over the edge yet.

"Carolyn wouldn't do that," Hazel finally said. "She isn't that kind of person."

"People respond differently to life situations. What did that restaurant mean to her?"

When Hazel looked away, Callum already had his answer. The restaurant had meant everything to Carolyn.

"That's why I felt so terrible," Hazel said.

And Carolyn had seemed gracious and forgiving. Even accepting, maybe overly so. "Let's talk to her again. Maybe keep an eye on her."

"You mean...do surveillance on her?"

"Yes."

After a while she shook her head. "I don't know. I can't believe she'd do something like that."

"Let's hope not. Let's hope Carolyn is not somehow associated with the killer."

"What if whoever you saw out there wasn't Carolyn and was just waiting for someone else?"

That was possible, but Callum wouldn't take any chances.

"I need to be sure, okay?" He met her eyes in a silent plea to heed him.

She blinked in concession. "Okay." Then she gave him a faint smile that told him she appreciated his careful concern.

He heard his phone go off, indicating he had received a text message. It was from Kerry. She was five minutes out from the inn and she asked him to meet her in the parking lot.

After they each changed into normal clothes, he

went back into the main room. "You wait here," he said to Hazel. "There's another officer outside on guard. I'm going to go down and meet Kerry."

"All right." Hazel sounded distracted, possibly weighed down by thoughts of Carolyn retaliating.

Assured that Hazel would stay put and she'd be safe in the suite, Callum rode the elevator down and went outside.

He spotted Kerry getting out of her vehicle. He also searched for the mysterious SUV and didn't find it. The driver must have given up and gone for the day.

He looked around for any other signs of danger. A man wheeled his luggage toward the inn entrance and a car left the parking lot. Movement drew his attention to a tree off to the side of the front doors, where a man smoked a cigarette and looked back at him. He was about the same build as the man he had seen who'd shoved a body into his trunk. It was hard to say, though, because this man stood and the other had been in the car. Could they be the same man?

"Do you see that?" Kerry asked.

"Sure do." He looked like a stalker. A few months ago, a creep had stalked Marlowe until he'd been caught.

"Let's go see if he'll talk to us."

Callum started for the man with her by his side. The man continued to smoke and watch them.

Kerry took out her badge and showed it to him. "Detective Kerry Wilder. Are you staying here?"

The man glanced at Callum and back at her, blowing smoke out and then dropping his cigarette onto the ground.

"No. I'm waiting for someone."

"What's your name?"

"Joseph Smith."

"Do you have any ID?" Callum asked.

The man removed his wallet and showed them his driver's license. It said Joseph Smith but any person, even a man who stole cars and committed murder, could come up with a fake one.

"Who are you waiting for?" Kerry asked.

"No one who's staying here. We just agreed to meet in this parking lot because it's halfway between where we live."

"What is the person's name who you're meeting?" Callum asked.

"You a cop like her?" Joseph asked.

"No. There's been suspicious characters loitering around this inn."

Joseph didn't respond right away but then he said, "Her name is Eleanor and I'd rather not tell you her last name. She's married. I don't want to get her in trouble."

Callum halfway believed this guy. Just when he was about to interrogate him some more, a gunshot rang out and a bullet splintered the bark of the tree.

"Holy…!" Joseph dove for the ground as Kerry and Callum drew their weapons and took cover, she behind the tree trunk and he behind another nearby.

He searched the parking lot and saw no moving

vehicles or anyone inside a vehicle. Most notably, there was no sign of the SUV.

He spotted something in the trees surrounding the inn. "Over there!" He pointed.

Kerry nodded and yelled, "You stay here!" then sprinted for the trees.

Callum followed. He couldn't in good conscience allow her to track down a killer on her own. But she was the detective.

The shooter had a good head start, but he ducked behind a tree trunk and poked his head out to shoot at them. He missed Kerry by inches.

Callum fired back, forcing the man to retreat. He got a good enough look at him to know this person was bigger than the one in the SUV. Whoever this person was, he was very desperate to silence anyone who could track him down.

He and Kerry emerged from the trees where they had taken cover and ran to two others closer to their target.

The shooter fled. Callum didn't have a good shot, but Kerry did. She fired and must have gotten the man's leg because he stumbled and then limped away.

Callum lost sight of him in the trees, but they soon reached a clearing and the highway. An older model Camaro was parked at the side of the road and the shooter got inside. By the time Callum and Kerry broke free of the trees, he had the car racing away. Kerry took aim and fired twice, breaking the back window but missing the driver.

She stood on the side of the highway staring after the vanishing car, putting her gun away.

Callum did the same.

"He's a slippery one, isn't he?" she said.

"Why did he shoot at us?" Callum asked.

"He was trying to shoot you," Kerry said.

He had shot at Kerry, too. Had he gone insane?

The detective called in the incident, which would bring in other officers. "I've got something else to discuss with you. Why don't you come up so Hazel can listen in?"

"All right. Is there more going on between you two than a mad shooter?"

He walked with her up through the trees—all part of the landscaping of the inn's grounds. "Unfortunately, yes." He was more convinced of that than ever.

Hazel heard the door open and looked up from the book she had been reading. She had to keep her mind off Evie. Kerry followed Callum into the suite.

Hazel stood from the sofa as they approached. "Did you find out who was out there?"

"That SUV was gone but someone started firing at us," Callum said.

"We were questioning a man who was standing outside the inn looking suspicious when we were shot at," Kerry added.

Hazel looked from her to Callum, confused as to who could have shot at them. "Was it the person in the SUV?" Maybe they had parked somewhere else.

Callum shook his head. "No. I'm sure of it. The gunman was bigger than the person in the SUV. I'm sure they're two different people."

"The person in the SUV is watching you?" Kerry asked. "Is it the stolen one from before?"

"No, this one was a charcoal gray and that other one was black. I didn't get a plate number, but I don't think that person is the same as the shooter. It's just suspicious. The gray SUV was parked out there a long time."

Kerry nodded. "Well, let me know if something changes or you see it parked out there again. And try to get a plate number. If it's someone different than our shooter, then maybe they won't be as careful." She glanced at Hazel. "Like, if it's someone you know." Looking back at Callum, she said, "I'll keep an undercover cop outside. I would suggest going somewhere else to stay, but given how brazen the shooter is, he will most likely come back. We could catch him if you keep drawing him here."

Callum told Kerry about Carolyn.

"Then your suspicion is definitely warranted. She may seem rational to your face but you never know what she's thinking or doing when no one is around."

Hazel didn't like imagining Carolyn capable of stalking her or something more, but she would keep an open mind.

"I should get going," Kerry said. "It's a really busy day." She stopped at the door. "Hey, did you have any luck tracking down Nan Gelman?"

Judging by Callum's frown, he hadn't done anything yet and felt bad. "I'm sorry, with everything going on…"

"It would be great if you could do that."

"I'll see what I can come up with in the next few days for you about Nan."

"Thank you," Kerry said. With that, Kerry left.

Alone with Callum, Hazel began to get uncomfortable, as she usually did, because she had such a hard time controlling her attraction to him. He was just so nice to look at. She even loved the sound of his manly voice. And she couldn't forget the frequent reminders of how good they were together in bed.

"I've got to cook some meals. Can you start looking for this Nan person?"

"I need access to some systems through work. I can call Charles and get something going."

Hazel went into the kitchen to start cooking, ever aware of Callum as he made a call to Charles, who must have been his boss. She listened to him make a request for remote access and Hazel gleaned from the call that Charles would have what he needed delivered later that day. Just like that, he'd be connected.

Callum sat on the sofa and saw her book. Picking that up, he read the title, then the back cover. "You like thrillers?"

"I like any action-packed murder mystery." She watched a lot of the murder case shows on television.

"I like those, too."

She sneaked a look at him. Pretty soon they'd be watching television together like a couple who'd been together for years. It already felt like she knew him that well.

He put the book down and flipped channels, stopping on a local one showing a reddish-blond-haired woman with blue eyes talking on a news program. She stood in front of the Colton Oil offices, so Hazel assumed she was a member of the family. She was quite attractive and looked to be in her late forties. The banner beneath her image read Selina Barnes Colton, VP and Public Relations Director of Colton Oil.

"Ace Colton is innocent until proven guilty," she said to a group of reporters.

"Have you seen or spoken to him since he's become a suspect?" a reporter asked.

"No, I have not, and I am sure he will be exonerated very soon." She flashed a megawatt smile for the cameras.

Hazel got the impression that she liked attention. She did not sound very sincere. One look at Callum and she knew he had similar sentiments about the woman.

She gave a wave to the reporters and walked like a movie star to her Mercedes—a much, much, much more expensive one than Hazel drove. Hazel experienced a few seconds of envy but she knew she would never be happy with that kind of lifestyle. Just looking at the woman gave her more than enough information. That woman thrived on attention and material things, expensive things, unattainable things for most people. Hazel thrived on her daughter and the everyday routine. She paid no heed to what strangers observed in her. They either accepted her or they did not. No bother to her.

Caring about all that would take too much energy. Energy better spent on what truly mattered. Evie. And real life. Real relationships.

Meeting genuine people was rare. Something to be cherished. Dear friends didn't come along at will.

Neither did meeting Mr. Right...

She saw Callum's expression had grown stormier.

Hazel finished with her recipe and put the freezable casserole into the oven. Cooking always lulled her into a state of artistic creation. She believed that the activity warded off stress and prolonged life because of that.

As she finished putting the food she had prepared into containers, she noticed Callum half-heartedly watching the newscast.

She put the Tupperware containers into the freezer, barely fitting them, and decided to delay cleaning the kitchen.

Going to where he sat, she plopped down beside him. "Everything okay?"

She saw his tension release. He leaned back and sighed. "Selina is kind of a loose cannon, in my opinion."

"Who is she to you?"

He let out another stress relieving breath. "Sorry. Selina Barnes Colton. She's vice president and director of public relations at Colton Oil. Also, my father's second ex-wife."

The way he said that piqued Hazel's curiosity. "Not well liked among the family?"

He grunted and looked at her. "No. My mother hates her. None of my brothers and sisters care for her much, either. We always were suspicious of her hold over him, why he keeps her on at Colton Oil."

Hazel saw him drift off into reflection. "She seems very good at her job. She put on a good show on that news segment. She might come across as lofty but I bet people buy into her game."

His demeanor smoothed some more and he looked at her again, this time much more warmly. "Yes, that is exactly how I would describe her. And I do think she is good at her job, but I also think she has something on my father and that is why he had to keep her on as an employee. She creates a lot of friction there—or so I'm told."

"But she's good at her job," Hazel summarized for him.

"She is good at her job."

"And you and your brothers and sisters are stuck with her."

"We are stuck with her." He met her eyes with warm regard.

As their uncontrollable chemistry heated up, he stretched his arm out behind her.

After a few simmering, electrically charged moments had passed, he said, "Selina hasn't let it leak to the press that Ace was ousted from the board."

Hazel didn't understand the significance of that. "Why wouldn't you want anyone to know?" Anyone paying attention to Payne's shooting in the news would know Ace was a suspect.

"The company bylaws say only a Colton by blood can be CEO."

That certainly held significance, but she thought of something else that might hold even more. "He wasn't ousted because he is a suspect in your father's shooting. He was ousted because he isn't a Colton by blood?"

Callum turned his head, his eyes going all shrewd and sexy. "No one knows Ace was let go because of the bylaws. She's trying to protect the company."

"That's a good thing, right?"

"Yes. It would seem so. Although I don't trust Selina. I never have."

"What if she's the one who sent that email?" Maybe she had learned Ace wasn't a Colton by blood. But then why shoot Payne?

Hazel didn't think Ace had a strong enough motive to shoot Payne. All his father had done was remove him as CEO. Having thought about it that way, though, Hazel changed her mind. Maybe Ace did have motive. In the throes of bitter emotions of loss and betrayal, he could have snapped.

"What kind of relationship did Ace have with Payne?" she asked.

"Not bad. Dad can be tough and isn't one you'd want to cross, but Ace was his son in every way. Ace *is* his son."

His cell chimed, indicating a text message had arrived. He read it and then got up to go to his laptop on the table. His boss must have come through with a way to track down the woman named Nan.

She followed, sitting beside him, seeing him navigate from his email to a browser. "What are you doing?"

"I couldn't find her in a regular search. She doesn't work as a nurse anymore, from what I can tell. Charles found a good way to search the web."

"What is that? A search engine?"

"No, it's not a search engine like what you're accustomed to using. It's more like a repository of archived data. It accesses content that search sites can't or that have removed the information because it is old. Hundreds of times more in volume."

That sounded intriguing.

"How can it do that?"

"They're databases, not websites. It's content that is invisible to normal search engines."

She watched as he typed in Nan's name, which produced a daunting amount of results. Callum didn't seem bothered. He worked intently.

In just a few minutes he brought up a file that looked like a photo of announcements. He scrolled to a twenty-year-old wedding announcement for Nancy and Herman Hersh. In the text, Nancy's maiden name was listed: Gelman.

"You found her!" Hazel exclaimed, amazed and impressed.

"Maybe." He went back to searching. "Nancy Gelman might not be our Nan Gelman."

The Dark Web had brought forth information on

a Nancy Gelman. Callum needed to find a link to Nan the nurse.

After a few more minutes he found the obituary of Samuel Gelman that listed the surviving family, with Nancy Hersh as one of them. He did additional searches and found that Nancy Hersh was the same person as Nan Gelman, a nurse who'd worked in the maternity ward at Mustang Valley General Hospital.

"She lives three towns over, in Mountain Valley," Callum said. "She's not related to the Gelmans from forty years ago that Kerry found in the census, though."

"We should tell Kerry."

While Callum called the detective, she called to check on Evie. She missed her daughter so terribly.

"Kerry is unavailable." He looked at Hazel after he hung up and she could see him contemplating going to see Nan himself. What could it hurt? They would help the investigation if they did and also save time.

"Let's go," Hazel said.

Nancy Hersh lived in a neighborhood one would expect of an average, everyday working family. Neat and tidy, green grass and no rundown vehicles or junk lying around. Callum walked with Hazel up to the door and rang the bell.

No one answered, so he rang the bell again.

Still, no answer. No one was home. After 6 p.m., it was late enough in the day that someone should be there after work.

"You looking for Nancy and Herman?" a woman called from the house next door.

Callum looked there and walked with Hazel into the woman's front yard. In jeans and an Arizona Cardinals T-shirt, the neighbor was in her forties with dark hair and rectangular glasses. He'd take advantage of her willingness to talk.

"Yes."

"They went to Europe. Just left yesterday. Won't be home for ten more days. Asked me to keep an eye on the place." She eyed them suspiciously. "Who are you?"

"They don't know us. We were hoping to ask Nancy a few questions," Callum said.

"About what?"

Was the woman being nosy or did she plan on reporting back to Nancy when she returned? Callum wasn't sure how much to reveal at this point. If Nancy had switched babies all those years ago when she worked at the hospital, had she suddenly vanished out of fear of prosecution—if she *was* the one who switched the babies? And why would anyone do that in the first place?

"We're reporters doing a story on the history of Mustang Valley General Hospital," Hazel said.

Callum inwardly cheered at her cleverness. "There was a fire there and we heard that Nancy was working around that time."

The woman's mouth spread into a smile. "Reporters, huh?"

She seemed happy that her friend and neighbor

would get a little notoriety for a story about a historic hospital.

"We're freelancers, but yes, the article would appear in the paper," Hazel said.

And again, Callum was captivated by her ingenuity. He had a sudden urge to do something romantic with her tonight. Maybe dinner in a dimly lit restaurant followed by a quiet night at the inn.

"We'll come back when she's home."

"I can tell her you stopped by," the woman said as they headed back for the car. "What're your names?"

Callum waved farewell and didn't answer, hoping the woman wouldn't grow suspicious again.

"Why don't we grab dinner while we're here?" he asked when they were in the car. "I know a great place." He knew they hadn't been followed, so he felt safe in spending a little quality time with Hazel. He wouldn't think about what that meant for the near future, how it might bring him closer to her.

"All right." She smiled over at him, the whole beautiful presentation sending sparks shooting through his chest.

Hazel was still floating on air after dinner. They had talked about opinions on politics and religion. They shared a lot of the same views.

At the hotel, she walked with him toward the entrance and saw a toddler with her mother. Wearing a cute pink dress with white tights, the girl laughed up at her mother, who crouched before her in the stroller.

Hazel could see and feel the love. Reminded of Evie at that age and younger, a pang hit her. A glance at Callum told her he had fallen into regret, likely thinking of Annabel.

"Evie was so adorable at that age," she said. "I wish I could have recorded the first time she said 'Mommy.' We were at the grocery store and she stared at my face like she always did. I have never seen a kid study faces the way she did. All of the sudden, when I was picking out some apples, I heard, 'Mommy.'" She smiled and a gush of love suffused her.

Callum chuckled. "I wish I could have been there. I can imagine it, though."

"All those moments happen when you least expect them. Except when she learned to walk. I taught her and she picked up on it pretty quickly, taking those first stumbling steps." Now she chuckled.

Callum opened the door for her and they entered the hotel. It was late, so they'd booked a room at this place rather than drive back late at night. The place was a nice one but not a five star like the Dales Inn.

She saw him reflecting again, his lightness gone.

"Are you thinking about Annabel?" she asked.

He turned to her as they headed for the bar. "About what I missed out on."

"You could always have another family, with someone else." With her…

They checked in and then walked to the elevators.

She stepped inside and faced him. He stood before her, still somber over what she had said earlier.

She wondered if he was pondering having a baby with her.

"The more time I spend with you and Evie, the more that seems like a possibility," he said.

"The more you feel you can?" she asked.

After a few seconds, he nodded. "Yes."

She met his heated gaze and stepped toward him. Deliberately avoiding thinking about what would happen when the case was solved, she put her hands on his face and kissed him.

She didn't mean for it to turn into a firestorm, but the instant their lips touched, passion flared and they kissed fervently. That made her glad she had gone on the Pill.

The elevator doors opened and that broke them apart.

Hazel saw an elderly couple waiting on the floor outside. They looked shocked.

Callum took Hazel's hand and led her down the hall to their door.

As he swiped the keycard to their room, she moved in front of him, not able to wait. She put her hands on his face again and kissed him. His hands flattened on her lower back and he pulled her against him.

Pushing the door open, he walked forward and she backward into the room, bumping into the door as it swung closed.

Hazel began to unbutton his blue shirt, spreading the material aside to put her hands on his bare chest. He pulled up her blouse and she moved back to lift her arms. He tossed that to the floor and removed his shirt. Then he unclasped her bra and she sent that to the floor as well.

Callum cupped her breasts. "I will never get tired of looking at these."

She liked the sound of that. *Never.* That implied a future.

He returned to kissing her, caressing her nipples as he did.

She ran her hands over his muscular chest and abdomen, then around to his back and up to his shoulders.

Callum lifted her and stepped to the bed, letting her down. He unbuttoned her jeans and she pushed them off her legs, along with her underwear, while he got out of his.

Both of them naked, he crawled on top of her. She wrapped her arms around him as he resumed kissing her.

Hazel lost herself in the feel of her hands on his skin, roaming down his back to his rear. Ending the kiss, he just looked down at her. The wonder of all this entranced her, too.

At last he kissed her again, and she opened her legs as he sought to enter her. For long, slow moments they moved together. Each gentle penetration stirred her senses higher and higher, until they both climaxed at the same time.

Afterward, he pulled her beside him and held her, kissing her forehead.

"What the hell is happening with us?" he asked softly. Although he swore, he sounded bewildered.

"I don't know."

She didn't admit aloud that this could be the makings of true love, and she sensed him doing the same.

Chapter 10

Callum stepped into the lobby of the Dales Inn, holding Hazel's hand. He had taken it after they left the car, ignoring the realization that the action had been automatic, driven by his affection for her and the passionate night they had shared. He also didn't want to hurt her by abruptly letting go.

The reception desk was busy. It was close to checkout time, and people rolled luggage toward the exit and away from the reception desk. People's voices mixed with a ringing telephone. A lone man walked toward the exit with no luggage. Something about him looked familiar. He had on sunglasses and a Stetson. Wrangler jeans and cowboy boots completed the cowboy ensemble.

The man looked at Callum and both of their steps slowed.

Callum knew this man. He approached and when he saw his jawline and nose in more detail he recognized Ace.

"Ace?" Callum checked out his brother. Ace would normally be seen in very expensive suits. About the only thing cowboy about him normally was his slightly unruly light brown hair.

"Yes. Callum." He leaned in for a quick manly hug. "Good to see you. I didn't know you had a new girlfriend." Ace looked at Hazel.

"This is Hazel Hart," Callum said.

She smiled and shook his hand. "Hello."

"From what I can see, Callum is the lucky one."

"Thanks for the compliment," Hazel said.

And Callum had to agree. He was the lucky one. Or not, if things fell apart.

"What are you doing here?" Callum asked.

Ace sighed his frustration. "I can't believe this is happening to me. I didn't shoot Dad."

Although Callum didn't believe his brother would kill anyone, he often wondered if it was possible Ace had fallen into a rage and acted impulsively. A lot of murderers went to prison that way. They seemed like normal, everyday, rational people but something happened to make them lose control momentarily and in seconds the deed was done. They killed and instantly wished they could undo the act.

"Dad had a long list of enemies," Callum said. "I wouldn't even know where to start to look for suspects." That's why he was a bodyguard and not a detective.

"I can't risk coming out of hiding. There is too much publicity." Ace glanced around as he must do all the time. "I'm going out of my room to get food. Other than that, I stay hidden. I'm a little worried you recognized me."

"I'm family. Anyone who doesn't know you well wouldn't."

"There are rumors all over Rattlesnake Ridge Ranch and my condo, so I'm staying at the Dales Inn until all the nonsense dies down. I'm half tempted to leave town, even though the cops told me not to. I cannot be arrested."

"You should be fine if you lay low," Callum said.

Ace didn't look convinced. "I miss it," Ace said. "Running Colton Oil. It's in my blood." He stopped as though catching himself. "Even if Colton blood isn't running through me, I am a Colton."

Having been raised by Coltons and then entering into the world of Colton Oil, Ace's entire life revolved around the family name. Callum felt for him, that he faced losing so much.

"No argument from me," Callum said. "You're my brother no matter what." Even if his instinct said Ace didn't shoot Payne and he ended up being wrong, Ace would always be his brother.

"I appreciate the support, brother." Then he glanced at Hazel. "What are you doing here?"

"Someone is after Hazel. She and her daughter

witnessed a murder." He went through a brief explanation, Ace listening.

"You're working," Ace said when he finished.

"In a way, yes."

"I saw you holding hands," Ace said. "So, it must be more than work."

"In a way," Hazel said, mimicking Callum's response.

Ace laughed, low and brief. "Love at first sight?"

Callum didn't have a comeback for that. Hazel must not have, either, because she also had nothing to say.

"It's about time you had a long-term relationship," Ace said. "It's been, what, almost five years now since Annabel?"

Callum nodded.

"I always wondered about that. She must have done a number on you. Weren't you the one who broke up with her?"

"It was mutual."

Callum half saw Hazel glance sharply at him. He shouldn't lie to his brother. Or his family. Not anymore.

"Actually, I lied about that, Ace."

Ace's expression sobered. "Why?"

"We didn't break up. She died in a car accident. I was protecting a witness testifying in the trial of someone who worked for a drug cartel. They found out I was dating Annabel and had her killed to intimidate me. Annabel was also pregnant."

Ace gaped at Callum in stunned silence.

"I'm sorry. I…couldn't talk about her." He looked at Hazel. "Not until I met Hazel."

Her eyes turned soft with deep gratitude and respect. He felt himself falling in love with her.

"Wow, Cal. I had no idea. You should have told someone."

He nodded. "Probably. But I just couldn't. It devastated me." Hell, it had changed him. He was not the same man as he was before that. He was a lot more cautious now. And better at his job. The one good thing that had come out of the experience.

"He blamed himself for her death," Hazel said to Ace. "She was murdered after the trial, when Callum was no longer watching over her."

"Then clearly it was not your fault."

"I should have checked out the suspect more. I should have known what kind of monster he worked for."

"You can't blame yourself for that. You aren't a cop. You're a bodyguard, and a damn good one." Ace did another check of the lobby and his eyes stopped short toward the entrance.

"Sorry to cut this short," Ace said. "I have to go now."

Callum followed his eyes and saw two police officers enter the lobby.

"You go back up to your suite. We'll bring food to you." Callum nudged his brother with a hand on his shoulder. "Hazel is a personal chef."

"I miss good food. The food here is good, but I mean my favorite restaurants."

Callum chuckled and gave his brother a pat on the back, letting him walk to the elevators. He wouldn't risk anyone exposing Ace.

"I hope I didn't sign you up for more work than you can handle," Callum said as they entered the suite.

Hazel walked in ahead of him, feeling him check out her butt. "It's a slow week. I have some pork chops to make today and that's pretty much it. I'd like some more to do."

"I'll pay you, of course. Can you come up with a week's menu?"

"What kind of food does Ace like?" she asked, turning in the living room to face him.

She saw him take in her face and chest. "He isn't picky. Seafood pasta, burgers, Mexican. Anything but Indian food."

"Easy enough. I'll write up a menu. I know a good weeklong plan."

Hazel used the same meals for certain types of people. In minutes she had a list and handed it to him.

"You're going to increase my revenue this month," she said. "There are perks to this relationship." She winked at him, making him want to take her into his arms and show her the other perks.

Hazel made a quick call to Evie, which she did each day. She went into the kitchen, hearing him phone Patsy. Once again she marveled over how quickly he could make things happen. He had people at his service with just a call. Money gave him that. As he talked to Patsy she admired his profile, from his sloping nose to his moving lips, and on down to his strong shoulders and chest, flat stomach...nice ass...and long, manly legs. He'd called Patsy for her. She had almost refused to let him pay her but she needed the money. And she also felt pampered and liked that.

Reminded of Ed, she cut short her too-trusting reaction. *Treat it like a business deal.* He wasn't asking her to prepare meals for his brother because he wanted her sexually. He'd asked for her business.

She started to prepare a pork chops recipe. Chops never turned out well if all you did was cook them in the oven. In culinary school she'd learned that the secret was to brine the pork first. Hazel had already done so and now got a pan out to sear the meat.

As she began to do that, Callum joined her in the kitchen. She retrieved the chops from the refrigerator, where they had been soaking in water and salt for three hours. Removing them from the solution, she placed them on a paper towel, flipping them to dry the other side.

Next, she brushed them with olive oil and then sprinkled them with garlic.

Callum joined in with the onion salt and she said, "Good," when he'd done enough on each chop.

She followed up with pepper, glancing up at him. His playful eyes caught hers. He enjoyed being close to her. The seasoning was just an excuse.

"If I stick with you I could learn how to cook," he said.

If he stuck with her? As in being girlfriend-boyfriend? She decided not to rein in her temptation to play along. This was too fun.

"I hope you're a fast learner, then." She let him interpret that any way he chose. She meant she hoped he'd learn to forgive himself for the deaths of his girlfriend and child and open himself up to new love. And quickly. Before Nate Blurge's murderer was caught.

"I fear you're the kind of woman who could make me one," he said.

He had interpreted what she had said exactly as she meant it. Tickled on the inside, she seared one side of the chops and then the other, feeling as hot as the pan right now.

After placing the chops on a pan, Callum put it into the oven. Then he straightened and faced her, the movement bringing him right before her.

She put her hands up against his chest, a reflexive reaction.

He didn't step away and she found herself melting into his eyes. The seconds ticked on but she was only aware of him and the heat rising.

"What's next?" he murmured.

"I…" Dazed by the fire coursing through her, she at first thought he referred to their close proximity.

"With the pork chops," he said.

"Oh." She breathed a laugh. "Three minutes on each side and then they're done. Then I need to make the vegetable. I already have the potatoes and gravy in the freezer."

Their room phone rang.

Hazel went to answer it. "Hello?"

"Hello," a man's voice said. "This is the front desk. We have a delivery here for Ms. Hart."

"Oh. A delivery?" She glanced at Callum, whose lighthearted expression turned to concern.

"Yes, ma'am."

"Okay. I'll be right down." She hung up and turned the stove off before going for the door. "There's something at the front desk for me."

Callum headed for the door ahead of her. "I'll go with you."

They took the elevator down.

In the lobby she walked with him to the front desk, where she already saw a vase full of flowers and a box of what had to be chocolates next to it.

"I take it you didn't send me those," she said, needing to keep the moment light.

"No, but maybe I should."

At the desk, she told the clerk her name. He slid the vase and box toward her.

Callum took the box and opened it. Inside were what appeared to be ordinary chocolates. She removed the card from the flowers.

Reading aloud, she said, "Thank you for preparing me all the wonderful meals. It's signed Abigail." She looked up at Callum. "That's my client who lives in the house where that man almost ran me and Evie over."

He took the box of chocolates. "We have to tell Kerry."

"Kerry...why?" Did he think Abigail sending these was significant? That had been her first thought, as well, but would the killer be this subtle? He had already tried to run her down and shoot her. He must know Evie wasn't with her now. If the chocolates were poisoned, he would only take out Hazel, not the star witness.

"It may be nothing but we have to be sure. If they turn out to be all right, I'll replace the box of chocolates."

She glanced at the flowers. Was there a way to poison those?

"I think we'd all be dropping dead already if those were casting off any toxins," Callum said, having read her thoughts.

"Abigail is a new client. If these are from her, it's good to know I won't be losing her."

"This doesn't seem like the killer's MO," Callum said. "It's more like what an ex-boss would do for revenge."

"Carolyn?" She still could not imagine her capable of murder. Why would she try to kill Hazel for leaving the restaurant? Even if she blamed her for her ruin, would she really resort to murder?

A few days later, Kerry called with the results of toxicological testing done on the chocolates and they came back negative. She'd also confirmed that Abigail sent them.

Callum asked Patsy to bring a replacement box to the front desk of the inn without Hazel knowing and was waiting for her call.

Hazel stood behind the kitchen counter, where she had worked for hours on a new order. The flowers, now in a vase, were still fresh on the dining table.

"Callum?" Hazel asked.

Judging by her tone he sensed a serious question was on the way.

"Yes?"

"Can I ask you something about Annabel?"

Yup, here they went. Mentally preparing himself, he said, "Yes."

She set down the knife she'd been using in the kitchen. "Do you still keep in touch with any of the friends you had together?"

What made her ask that? "We didn't really have any friends in common, only mine and hers."

"Why haven't you spoken with her parents in all these years?"

"They don't want to hear from me."

"You indicated that before, but I have my doubts. If anything, they'd be more upset that you didn't keep in touch. You were the last person to be close to her. You were going to have a baby together. Don't you think they'd like to talk to you? You could tell them things about her in the days before she died. Was she happy? Maybe some special moment you two had. They probably needed that and you abandoned them."

"I didn't abandon them. I got their daughter killed. Seeing me would only remind them of that."

"Now, see, there's where I think you're wrong. You said they invited you to the one-year memorial and you didn't go."

"I couldn't go."

"Right. You were out of the country, but you could have called and told them that."

He looked over at her, unable to refute her point. "Okay then, I couldn't have gone even if I was available."

"Now *that* I believe," she said. "You've been running all this time. You buried her and your emotions. You didn't even tell your own family about her death."

"I *couldn't*." Didn't she get it?

"But I bet you can now," she said quietly, gently.

It had been long enough now that he should be able to face Annabel's family. And funny how the thought of that wasn't as painful as it had been in the months after Annabel's death. He felt more open to the idea.

"It would help you move on, Callum," Hazel said. "And now that I have a vested interest in you, I encourage you to reach out to them."

She had a vested interest in him? He grinned over her choice in words.

"And I'm hoping you feel the same about me and will work on getting over Annabel's death."

She hoped he had a vested interest in her. Did he? He enjoyed her company. He felt an intense attraction to her. But he still couldn't think about any kind of long-term future with her.

His cell chimed and he was relieved for the interruption. He read a text from Patsy. The returned chocolates were downstairs.

"There's something for you at the desk again," he said to her.

"Again?"

"Maybe it's another admirer. Come on. Let's run down there."

She rinsed her hands and dried them and then adjusted one of the burners to low. Then she rode the elevator with him. In the lobby they were headed for the desk when he spotted a woman who looked vaguely familiar. She wore a baseball cap and sunglasses, but her hair was a blond bob. Carolyn. She wasn't dressed as smartly as when he'd first seen her. She wore jeans and a T-shirt today. Was she trying to disguise her appearance?

She turned her head and saw them. Callum pretended not to notice her and went to the desk with Hazel. The clerk gave her the new box of chocolates.

"Those are from me," Callum said. His voice sounded lower than normal and he had to attribute that to liking giving her something romantic.

Her mouth parted in surprise and she took them. "I didn't think you'd actually do this. Thank you."

He'd have to get her flowers, too, when the others wilted.

Carrying the box, she opened it a crack to retrieve

one, popping it into her mouth as she walked away from the counter.

Callum looked toward Carolyn. She watched them. Was she trying to monitor their movements? If so, she was doing a terrible job. He looked through the front windows to the parking area and saw a dark SUV.

Taking Hazel's hand, he steered her toward Carolyn. Might as well confront her. Maybe it would dissuade her from any future attempts to do whatever she might intend against Hazel.

"That's Carolyn over there," he said to Hazel.

She searched the room until her gaze came back to the woman in the cap. "She never dresses like that."

"I didn't think so."

Carolyn stood as they approached, awkwardly removing her sunglasses as though feeling caught. "Well, fancy meeting you here again."

"Carolyn," Hazel said. "Why are you here?"

"I'm waiting to meet the manager about an upcoming catering event."

"Who are you catering for?" Callum asked.

"It's a local business," she said, sounding blasé. "An all-day meeting."

He doubted she had to meet in person to discuss what needed to be done in preparation for a business meeting.

"Why are you still here?" Carolyn asked. "Is that man not captured yet?"

"No, unfortunately."

"Where is Evie?" Carolyn asked. "I never see you without her."

With Hazel's hesitation, Callum knew she was thinking twice about telling her former boss. "She's somewhere safe."

Carolyn eyed her peculiarly, as though not missing that Hazel had chosen not to tell her. "This whole thing must be so disruptive to your business. Without a kitchen to handle all that cooking."

"Oh, no. It hasn't slowed me down at all," Hazel said. "Our suite has a full kitchen and Callum has lined me up with new customers."

Callum wondered if she was aware of how unabashedly excited and happy she sounded to be so busy.

"He has, has he?" Carolyn looked over at him and then back at her.

"I'm supplying one of his brothers with food this week and that has already led to other customers."

Ace had recommended a few to Callum, who had made some calls. Hazel's business was thriving and would continue to do so.

"You always did seem charmed," Carolyn said with a hint of resentment. "Some people are just born with luck, aren't they? A great start to a new business and a handsome man to boot. Cute little girl. How do you do it? Is there a method?"

"I…" Hazel seemed perplexed. "I guess I just follow my heart."

"That's what I did and look where it got me."

Hazel studied her for several seconds. "Carolyn,

you aren't angry with me for leaving your restaurant, are you?"

Carolyn waved her hand through the air. "Of course not. I understand people have their own lives to live."

Her answer fell flat because she seemed to be overdoing her sugary tone.

"Yes, but my leaving put you in a difficult position. I wish you would have told me."

"You were busy doing your thing. People do that. They move on without a second thought to those around them. I'm sure you did what was best for you and your daughter."

"Carolyn. Maybe we should talk. You're angry with me."

Carolyn shook her head. "No. I just understand people."

"People in the restaurant industry can be brutal. Not just cantankerous customers, either," Hazel said. "Executive management and coworkers. It's a highly stressful environment for a career. That was one of the reasons I left it. I'm not in a restaurant environment anymore. Maybe you should consider doing something similar."

Carolyn scoffed. "You told me that was one of your reasons. You had a daughter to look after and wanted to be with her more. But that kind of choice won't work for me. I'm not a chef."

Did Carolyn now feel trapped in an unsatisfying career? She must prefer being the boss. Short of owning a restaurant, she'd still have to report to someone. Nobody liked that but most of them had no choice. Callum was lucky to have a boss who let him do his job and didn't inflict any ego-driven power trips on him.

"The manager must be running late," Callum said.

Carolyn turned to him and he saw that she recognized he didn't believe her.

"I'm early."

"I mean it, Carolyn," Hazel said. "We should talk."

Callum would not allow that unless he was right next to her. Second nature in his line of work was not trusting anyone, especially when there appeared to be a good reason not to. Why would Hazel suggest such a thing? Why did she want to talk to her? He got it that she had empathy for the woman, but maybe she was trying a little bit too hard.

"We have talked. I don't think there's anything left to say."

But maybe there was something to *do*. And what would that be? What would Carolyn do in retaliation for Hazel causing the demise of her business?

Chapter 11

Hazel went with Callum to check on his father. There was still no change in his condition. Callum wanted to sit in the room awhile. Hazel sat on the couch, her bodyguard in a chair beside the bed, just watching his father's still and pale face. Machines hummed around him and lines hung from Payne's body.

Hazel could see Callum genuinely needed another chance to be close to Payne Colton. His tense mouth and eyes said that his thoughts ventured beyond worry.

"Who besides Ace do police think may have shot him?" she asked.

He looked at her, coming out of his deep thoughts.

"They considered many, most in the family. They even considered Marlowe, since she is now CEO."

Hazel wondered if all of this was related to Ace being switched at birth. "It seems like too much of a coincidence that he was shot so soon after that email was sent about Ace not being a Colton by blood."

He nodded. "Yeah, I thought about that myself. We're all trying to figure out who switched him—and if that same person sent that email via the Dark Web. Marlowe and I tried to find hospital records, but a hospital administrator told us there was a fire on Christmas morning, the morning Ace was born. All the records were destroyed. We thought it too much of a coincidence that the fire broke out then."

"The person who did the switch must have set it," she said.

"Yes. It would seem that way. What we all can't understand is, why anyone would switch a healthy baby with one who wasn't?"

"The real Colton baby wasn't healthy?"

"No. He wasn't doing well. That's why Ace was called a Christmas miracle, because none of his symptoms were present the next day."

Further proof—if the DNA wasn't enough—that Ace had been switched. Someone really unbalanced must have done it. Hazel could see no other motive for Ace to shoot Payne than anger over being cast out of Colton Oil. Whoever had shot Payne had to have another reason—one related to the baby switching. Maybe she was wrong, she was no detective, but the motive had to be more complicated than that.

"Is there any evidence supporting Ace's innocence?" she asked. All the times she'd encountered him, he had not struck her as a violent man. She had a good barometer when it came to judging people. In the last two weeks they'd stopped by his room four times. Ace had never been anything but kind and gracious when she and Callum had delivered food.

"Not really," he said. "There's video footage showing a person who's around five-nine wearing a ski mask and black clothes near the crime scene. If it's a man he's not very big. Ace also doesn't own a gun. If anything, the evidence points toward him. It might not be Ace in the video but Ace had the resources and the motive to hire someone to shoot Payne. There's no video showing him coming home the night of the shooting but there is video showing other Coltons arriving home at the mansion."

"So, there was nothing wrong with the surveillance equipment." If Ace claimed to be home, which he must be doing, then the video evidence contradicted that. "And then there's the threat that the board all witnessed."

"Yes, the threat. And a cleaning woman named Joanne Bates, who found Payne's body, heard someone say *mom* just before he was shot." He looked back at his father, clearly frustrated that his brother had to be in such a perilous situation.

Hazel stood and went to him, putting her hand on his shoulder. He looked up and put his right hand over hers. Warm tingles spread through her as their gazes met and locked. She could feel him returning what she felt. With just a touch and the invisible energy linking them in a look, she fell into the magic of their chemistry.

If Evie had been there, she'd have acted as a buffer. Without her, there was none. Hazel might as well be floating through rapids toward a waterfall ahead. As soon as she reached the edge, there'd be no turning back.

Callum spent the next two days thinking about what he and Hazel had discussed about going to talk with Annabel's parents. Avoiding them had been a burden in and of itself. Not telling anyone about Annabel's death had, too. He had to agree it was long past due that he go and see them.

He had just finished making a delivery for Hazel. Driving in the car gave him more time to solidify his decision. He had also had time to make a few calls.

Entering the suite, he found Hazel relaxing on the sofa with her feet up. Something smelled really good.

"What's for dinner?"

"Truffled bay scallops with celery purée, buttery potatoes and snap peas."

"You're going to make me fat." He went to her, bent and planted a kiss on her mouth. It was something he had never done before—come home and kiss her, first thing. She looked up at him with startled but heated eyes.

"I made arrangements to fly to San Francisco to go see Annabel's parents. I decided not to tell them I'm coming."

After surprise turned to a warm glow of appreciation, she reached up and touched his cheek. "That's good, Callum."

"You're coming with me." He wouldn't let her out of his sight. "We'll be safer if we aren't here anyway."

"How long will we be there?"

"I got open tickets so we can come back when we need to. In case they aren't home when we go there."

"You want me to be with you? I don't think—"

"Yes. I want you there. You're the one who helped me get to this point. I want you with me."

She tipped her head back, seeking his mouth. Still bent over, he obliged and kissed her. He kept his mouth pressed to hers, feeling her breath and the sparks that always started with just this.

Reluctantly lifting his head, he looked into her sultry eyes. "Keep that up and you're going to rope this cowboy in."

She smiled. "You're not a cowboy."

He chuckled. "I can be for you." Seeing her smile slowly fade, he knew some sobering thought had caused it, something about the two of them. He walked around the sofa and sat beside her. "What's the long look for?"

She sighed and snuggled closer to him. He put his arm around her, feeling this was so right.

"I can see a weight has been lifted off you," she said.

It has. "I do feel that way. It feels good."

"I love this," she said. "You and me relating like we're a couple, like this could last."

He hadn't thought much about the future. He had only acted on how good it felt to look forward to resolving something he hadn't thought bothered him as much as it had.

"Well, what if things don't go the way you expect in San Francisco? What happens after this euphoria fades and you begin to think about how serious you and I are becoming?"

"Are we becoming serious?" He wasn't so sure. They had great sex. How could they know that would translate into compatibility in every other way? How did anyone know that without spending months, or even years, together?

She moved back from him. "Do you have any feelings for me?"

He knew he was falling for her and thought she was extremely beautiful. More. There was something about her that was different from any other woman. "I enjoy being with you." And he truly meant that. He loved spending time with her and Evie. "We seem to be hitting it off really well. You make me feel good and I hope I make you feel the same. So, yeah, I'd say I have feelings for you."

He didn't want to ask if she had feelings for him. He didn't want to know right now. What if something happened to her or Evie? He cringed with even the suggestion. He could not go through that again. Not ever. And given her situation, she was in a lot of danger. Something could easily happen to her.

Best to keep his distance—at least for a little while longer.

* * *

After they landed in San Francisco, Hazel drove with Callum to their hotel. They checked in and then Callum drove their rental to Annabel's parents' house. She was probably as nervous as he was, but for a different reason. He was about to face the biggest demon from his past and she would find out if there was any hope for them as a couple.

On the way, she called Evie. Her brother answered.

"Hey, it's me," she said.

"Hazel. How are you?" Owen asked. "Is everything okay? I was about to call you to check."

"We're doing fine. We are going out of town for a little bit, hopefully to find information. How's Evie?"

"She's good. Keeping busy."

"Is that Mommy?" Hazel heard her daughter almost screech in excitement. She missed her so much.

"She's about to grab the phone from me." Owen chuckled as Hazel listened to him hand the phone to Evie.

"Mommy?"

"Yes. Hi, honey, how are you?" Being without her had been a lot harder than she thought. Not having that bundle of energy around all the time created a big hole.

"I miss you. When are you coming to get me?"

"I can't yet, but I hope to real soon. Are you having fun?" She would try to steer her daughter away from talk of when she could go get her and bring her home.

"Yes. We went on a picnic and the movies. I got to see Tinkerbell."

"Oh yeah?" Adoration and love filled her to overflowing. And gratitude for her brother keeping Evie entertained.

"Yeah. And they took me to work. I got to ride in a police car."

"Wow. That's exciting." Owen wouldn't have taken her on any emergency calls. He must have just given her a ride.

"Mommy?"

"Yes, sweetie?"

"I want to be a police girl when I grow up."

Evie had been getting a lot of exposure to policewomen, first Kerry and now Jessica. "That's a good profession. You'd make a fine one. And you're already getting experience." Hazel believed that children could not get enough encouragement. It allowed them to focus more on the positive than the negative, what they could do as opposed to what they couldn't.

"I like Jessica. She bosses all the boys around."

Hazel laughed and saw Callum pull to the side of the street. They had arrived at Mark and Loretta's home.

"She's a good role model for you then. I've got to go, Evie. You be good for me."

"Okay, Mommy."

Hazel would never get tired of her kiddie voice, high and sweet. She'd miss that when Evie grew up. "I love you."

"Love you, too."

Hazel didn't hear any disconnect and in the next couple of seconds her brother came back on. "Hey," he said.

"She sounds really good."

"Yeah. She's a good kid. You're doing an amazing job with her."

"Give her a kiss and a hug for me."

"Will do. Are the police any closer to catching that shooter?"

"No. We're trying to track down information on the victim and hoping that will lead to something. All we know so far is he liked to flirt and he went to a bar a lot. The sooner we find out more, the better." She wanted Evie back by her side.

"Well, don't worry about Evie. She's warm, safe and dry here."

Warm, safe and dry. "I like that. Thanks, Owen."

"Take care."

She ended the call and looked over at Callum, who must have been watching her and listening the whole time. He had a soft expression, his eyes full of admiration or maybe envy. For a man who shied away from mothers and children, he sure seemed to yearn for exactly that type of family life.

"You ready?" she asked.

"Yes." He got out of the car and so did she.

They walked to the house, a three-thousand or so square foot two-story home. A rock water fountain bubbled beside the front door. Callum rang the bell. After a few moments a lanky man with a headful of gray hair appeared. He looked from Hazel to Callum and froze. He was surprised to see him.

"Hello, Mr. Rubio."

"Why are you here?" Mark asked.

"I'd like to talk if you're okay with that."

Mark Rubio stared at him awhile.

"This is Hazel Hart," Callum said without any further explanation as to why she was there with him.

"Who's here, Mark?" a woman called from inside.

A remarkably youthful woman appeared, blue eyes widening and then going rather chilly as she stopped beside her husband.

"Well, you're here, so you may as well come in." Mark moved aside.

"Thank you." Callum stepped in, putting his hand on Hazel's lower back.

She wasn't sure if the contact gave him reassurance or if it was an automatic gesture. Either way, she felt the touch all the way to her toes.

The house was clutter-free and painted in shades of gray and earthy tones with white trim. Mark led them into a formal living room toward the front of the house. Hazel got the distinct impression that was no mistake, as though Annabel's father did not want to welcome them into their home.

Mark and Loretta stood on the opposite side of the entry, facing Callum and Hazel.

"First, I want to apologize for not coming to see you sooner," Callum said. "When you sent that invitation to the year memorial of her death, I should have at least called you."

"You vanish from our lives as though Annabel didn't matter one bit and you expect us to believe you? You discarded her like trash. Were you glad she was gone? That's how it seemed to us."

Callum shook his head emphatically. "I never meant to make you think that. I just... I just couldn't..."

Mark's brow creased in confusion. "You had nothing to do with her murder."

"I should have protected her. I could have."

"How?" Mark asked.

Callum pinched the bridge of his nose and then let his hand drop. "I should have known she would still be in danger after I finished protecting that witness."

"You did your job."

"You should have been with us during that time," Loretta said. "You abandoned us. You were all we had left of her."

"I'm sorry." Callum breathed out. "I'm here now. I'm here the soonest I could be, largely thanks to this woman here." He put his arm around Hazel. "She helped me see what I had been doing, which was burying extreme pain."

"What do you think we were going through?" Loretta asked. "We lost our daughter and our grandchild. When you vanished we lost a son-in-law."

Callum hadn't married Annabel, but they must have thought of him as part of the family.

"He didn't tell anyone in his family Annabel died," Hazel said.

"No one?" Loretta asked, incredulous.

"I couldn't."

Loretta stepped forward then. "Oh, you poor man." She touched his face. "You should have come to see us. You could have talked to us about it. We needed that with you."

"I know that now. I'm sorry."

"This doesn't make things all right with us," Mark said. "You caused our grief to be worse by not being with us."

Hazel thought that was a little over-the-top. Mark must not be a very forgiving man, but his wife was.

"I know it's taken me too long to come and see you. If there's anything you want to talk about, I'm here now."

Loretta stepped back. "There is something I have wondered all this time." She folded her arms. "Annabel told us about the baby the day after she found out, the day after you both found out. But I didn't get to talk to her much before she died. She came to see me once and we talked about how good things were going between you two. She didn't know at that time whether you were having a boy or a girl, but I know she had an ultrasound scheduled."

Hazel wished she could give the three some privacy. She felt this was a very personal moment.

"She was at twenty weeks," Callum said. "There was no sign of a penis and the doctor said we were having a girl."

Loretta covered her mouth with her hand as a sob wrenched her.

Hazel lowered her gaze, feeling she intruded too much.

"She was thrilled," Callum said. "So was I."

Hazel looked at him and became captivated by the light in his eyes, the slight curve of his lips the memory brought. That had been a magical moment for him. Hazel remembered when that day had come for her. *Magical* didn't come close to describing what seeing the miracle of life could do to a person.

As she realized the depth of his emotional injury, the weight of the risk to her heart settled in. His journey to healing wasn't over. And she had been instrumental in guiding him onto this path. She might be the rebound woman.

The image of Evie's gap-toothed smile pierced her. Her innocent eyes. Her tiny, soft-skinned fingers. The way she sometimes skipped instead of walking. When she talked to bumblebees and ladybugs. Not spiders. Although she did respect the aphid eaters… She didn't want to involve her child in a tenuous relationship with a hopeful father figure who had so much weight to bear. But the more time she spent with Callum, the more she felt like it was out of her control.

Chapter 12

Callum knew Hazel had suffered at least some tension during that visit.

He might be a brawny workingman, but he did have a sensitive side. He was grateful for her support despite how she must have felt like an intruder. And hearing about his and Annabel's special moment could not have been easy.

She had been quiet all the way to the hotel near the airport and now surfed channels on the television. Their flight back to Arizona was in the morning. Callum couldn't explain his need to make it up to her, to tell her that Annabel's memory didn't loom large as much as it used to. A voice said Hazel mattered more but that scared him, so he didn't give it any credence.

Going to the suite phone, he called room service and ordered champagne with strawberries and requested a delayed dinner of steak and crab. When he hung up and turned to Hazel, he saw her looking at him peculiarly.

"I figured we could use a nice dinner tonight," he said.

Her eyes narrowed.

"Okay, I figure I owe you at least that, if not more, for what you did for me today."

"Me? I didn't do anything."

"You were there for me." He walked over to where she sat on the sofa and took a seat right next to her. Taking the remote, he searched for a classical music station and found one playing a piano dominant tune.

After a few minutes, she said, "I know what you meant about seeing the sex of the baby for the first time."

"Were you alone when you saw it?" he asked.

"Yes. My family was in Colorado. But I sent them copies of the sonogram."

"That kind of thing bonds the parents together," he said.

"So I gathered." She inched away from him on the sofa. "You and Annabel had a special thing going."

He had brought up the bonding on purpose. He intended to lead into what he really needed to say.

"We did bond over the baby, but that didn't change the way either one of us felt about each other. I told you I would like to believe I loved her, but after all this time and much reflection, I know I didn't love her as much as I could love a woman." He wouldn't say how he knew that. He knew because he could love Hazel ten times more. "I loved her enough to marry her and have a family, but at some point, it would have become clear that she wasn't the one for me, and I would always have wondered who the right woman would have been."

"Would you have stayed in the marriage?"

"With children involved? Yes. Annabel was a good person. Honest, full of integrity. There would have been no good reason to leave her."

"Other than not being happy," Hazel said.

"I would have been happy enough with her. It's not like she made me miserable, nor do I think she ever would have." There were different degrees of happiness. People could find great joy even if they married someone they weren't madly in love with. As long as there was loyal companionship and friendship, marriage could work.

"I would have had plenty of good reasons to leave Ed, had he stayed and married me," Hazel said. "I'm not even sure I would have agreed to marry him."

Room service knocked and Callum let them in. The champagne was in an ice bucket and the strawberries in a bowl. The room service attendant put the tray on the coffee table. Callum tipped him and he left.

Going back to Hazel, he sat beside her. Leaning forward, he removed the bottle of champagne and easily and gently popped the cork, which didn't go flying. Setting that aside, he poured Hazel, then himself, some. Handing her a glass, he clinked his to hers.

"Here's to you being the amazing woman you are."

She smiled softly. "Thank you."

As she sipped, her golden-green eyes looked up at him suggestively, heatedly. When she lowered her glass, she said, "If you aren't careful, you might end up liking me too much to leave me when this is all over."

He'd rather not go there yet. "Maybe. I prefer to take it one day at a time."

"Me as well." She took a strawberry from the bowl and put it to his mouth.

He ate it and then took one for her, feeding her a strawberry.

"Mmm, there is something about strawberries and champagne," she said.

"It's the pairing of the sweetness in both." He sipped some champagne.

"What were you like before Annabel?" Hazel asked.

He wasn't sure what she wanted to know. "With women? The same."

"No, did you date a lot? My guess is you had girls crawling all over you in high school. After that you must have dated a lot."

He hadn't thought of that since Annabel was killed. He had been very different. "I did date a lot."

"Were you popular in high school?"

"I was a quarterback. I wouldn't say I was the

most popular. I didn't get into school politics. That crowd seemed more popular."

She breathed a laugh, clearly disagreeing.

"What about you?" he asked.

"I was popular. I was a cheerleader and I dated the quarterback. He and I were king and queen at our senior prom."

"Do they still do that in school? Kings and queens." He grunted in humor. "Seems like another lifetime ago." He set aside his glass.

"Yes, and I'm only twenty-five."

More memories from that time came to him. He hadn't been popular with the good kids. He had run with a more rugged crowd.

"Back then I had more of a reputation as a bad boy," he said.

She nodded thoughtfully. "I can see that." She put her glass on the side table.

This conversation was far more interesting than sharing champagne and strawberries. "I started rebelling against my dad my sophomore year. That's when he began *prepping* me for joining the Colton Oil executives." He had not been executive material. Even as a kid he had always sought danger. Climbing trees. Riding motorcycles and mountain bikes. Rock climbing. Skiing. Anything exciting.

"I got into a lot of fights. Some of the other kids tried teasing me about being a Colton, a spoiled rich kid. Those kids usually got nosebleeds after I punched them. I almost was expelled. I think only my father's connections prevented that. He grounded me and tried reasoning with me, but I never listened. He never laid a hand on me but I bet he wanted to more than once."

"A bad boy. All because your dad wanted you to join Colton Oil?"

"Not just that. I aspired to a different existence. Something more earthy and adventurous."

"Hence the military and then personal protection." *Earthy and adventurous.*

He had never conveyed his life journey to anyone in that way. He left his thoughts to look at her, this magnificent woman. "I loved the navy, but not the discipline. Being a bodyguard suits me perfectly."

Hazel sat back and sipped her champagne, crossing one slender leg over the other. In admittedly selfish pleasure, he covertly took in the shape of her knee and the lines of her fit thighs and the side view of the curves of her butt.

"Mr. Callum Colton," she said, turning her head with just the right angle to give her eyes a sultry slant. "You are one sexy, successful man."

Her relaxed pose and flirtatious words and tone threw him. "And…you are…" What could he say? She had already trumped him. *She* was one sexy, successful woman. Taking a chance, he moved in, touching her cheek and kissing her.

He would have encouraged her for more but she drew back, almost flinching.

Opening his eyes, he searched hers.

After several seconds, she asked, "Would you ever be able to try having a family again?"

Her catching, whispered question speared him.

This conflict would not go away. She had been abandoned, pregnant with Evie, and he had lost the mother of his unborn child, and with her a baby girl he would never know.

He and Hazel had issues that meant they might never be able to work together to form a healthy, new relationship. Everything felt so good with her. Everything felt right and safe. But was it?

Callum could never go through what he'd gone through with Annabel ever again. He had to be honest here. People died. Hazel could die. Something could happen to both her and Evie. What if they had a child of their own? Something could happen to that child.

He imagined living with Hazel and Evie, having a blended family and living an everyday life together. Spending time in the evenings with them. Doing schoolwork. Going to bed every night with Hazel. He would fall in love with that life. He could already feel it to his core. And then, after growing more attached than he had ever been to Annabel, what if something tragic happened? Nothing and no one could predict life or what awaited everyone as time marched on.

"I don't know if I'm ready for that." Would he ever be?

His spirit plummeted as he saw Hazel's reaction. Her face hardened to disappointed stone and she lowered her eyes in sadness before getting up from the sofa.

"Good night," she said.

The urge to go after her nearly brought him to his feet. That urge, foreign in its powerful, primal need. *Go after her. Take her.* Never let her out of his bed. Ever.

But therein lay the problem.

He'd only just begun to confront the tragedy of his past. If not for Hazel, he would not have gone to see Annabel's parents. He had blocked all emotion where his ex-girlfriend was concerned. Nearly five years later he still wasn't over his loss. It was unfair to lead Hazel on, to let her believe he was ready for a future with her and Evie.

Evie.

Oh.

He could not, he *would* not, hurt that wonderful child—or her amazing mother.

Hazel hadn't liked Callum's answer yesterday, but there was little she could do about it. There was even less she could do about how she was beginning to feel about him. Conversation had been limited on the way back from San Francisco. Now they were back at the inn and Patsy arrived with another food delivery. With the help of two hotel staff members, the goods were unloaded on the kitchen island counter.

"Thank you, Patsy. You sure are indispensable for Executive Protection…and now me." She smiled.

Patsy gave a quick, "No problem," and turned to leave.

Odd, the woman seemed to be behaving differently than usual. She seemed awkward, as though something troubled her.

"Is everything all right, Patsy?"

"Yes, fine." She offered a half-hearted smile and left.

Hazel watched her go behind the hotel staffers and then turned to Callum, who sat at the dining room table in front of his laptop, digging up what he could on Nan, all the places she had lived, places she had worked, people she knew from her Facebook page and other social media sites.

"Patsy seems out of sorts today," she said.

He looked up. "How so?"

"I don't know. Does she have a happy home life?"

"As far as I know. She always seems happy to me."

"Hmm." She began putting food away, starting with the produce and perishables like milk. Next came the canned goods and other pantry items.

Lifting the jar of olive oil, her fingers came in contact with something grainy. Inspecting the jar, she saw traces of a white substance, a powdery film. And then she saw what appeared to be a fingerprint on the glass. Holding the jar closer to her eyes, she spotted undissolved white particles inside, floating in the olive oil. Twisting the cap, she found the seal had already been broken.

"Callum?"

He looked up again and then stood to come to her.

"This doesn't look good," she said.

He took the jar and placed it on the counter, then

bent to examine it. "It looks like it might be poisonous."

Patsy's edgy demeanor came back to her. No. One of Callum's agency's assistants?

"You said Patsy was acting strange?" Callum asked.

"Yes."

"Someone could have paid her to try and poison us."

"Not me, my clients," she said. "I would have used this oil for recipes to be delivered."

His mouth flattened in consternation. "That doesn't sound like something the killer would do. He'd want *you* dead. You and Evie. Evie isn't here and he can't find her. While he must be getting impatient, I doubt he'd go after your clients."

Well, Hazel could think of only one other person who had a motive to see Hazel's clients die. Carolyn.

The next day Kerry reported the jar of olive oil had been tested. The liquid had been poisoned. Kerry also let them know she'd picked up Patsy and now had her in custody. Callum took Hazel to the police station. She entered the observation room with Callum and watched Kerry interrogate the nervous woman.

"This will go much easier for you if you cooperate," Kerry said. "Now, I'll ask you again. Why did you put poison in the olive oil that was delivered to Callum Colton and Hazel Hart's room at the Dales Inn?"

"I didn't put poison in it," Patsy said, wringing her hands.

"Then you must know who did, because you were the one who purchased the oil and helped deliver it."

"I don't."

Kerry sighed. "I know you do. I have enough to arrest you right now. We have a fingerprint on the jar. My guess is, it's yours. Do you really want to take that chance?"

"It's not mine," Patsy said. "I just made the delivery."

"How can you be so sure?"

Patsy continued to wring her hands and now added chewing her lower lip to her edgy movements.

"Whose fingerprint could it be?"

"If I tell you, are you going to arrest me?"

"I can't guarantee anything, but maybe I can ask our DA, Karly Fitzpatrick, to see if we can work out a deal with you. We might be able to get you probation instead of prison time, especially since this is your first offense."

Chewing on her lip, Patsy flattened her hands on the table as she mulled over her options and the consequences of whatever decision she made.

"All right. It was Carolyn Johnson. She said she saw me make other deliveries to Hazel and offered to pay me to deliver the olive oil. She didn't say she was going to poison it, but I'd suspected she did something to it. I didn't think she'd actually try and murder anyone."

Hazel glanced at Callum. Surely Patsy would have known Carolyn had intended something terrible.

"How did she come in contact with you?"

"She saw me going in and out of the inn and approached me one day. She asked if I was close to Hazel and I said I didn't know her, I was an assistant, who brought them things they needed. She then asked if I could use a little extra cash to deliver something to her."

"How much did she pay you?" Kerry asked.

"Five hundred."

"Why did you do it?"

"I needed money. The agency doesn't pay me very much. They could afford to pay me more but they don't. I'm behind on my bills."

"I can't believe that," Callum said. "We pay all our employees top wages. What did you expect? Personal assistants don't make what executive bodyguards do."

"Desperate people do desperate things." Hazel was still reeling over her ex-boss trying to kill her clients. She must have intended for her to be accused of the murders. Revenge for causing her restaurant to fail? Since Carolyn had failed, Hazel should fail and her clients die?

"Is Kerry going to arrest Carolyn?" Hazel asked.

"If she can find her, I'm sure she will."

"You okay?" Callum held the station door for her as they walked to the rental.

She nodded. "Just shocked and disappointed."

She did seem pretty upset. Someone she had respected and might have even considered a friend or mentor had betrayed her in the worst possible way.

Today, they weren't in disguise, so extra precautions were in order. The emergency had prevented them from taking those precautions. He took care in looking around for potential threats.

No parked vehicles with anyone sitting inside.

No strangers walking dogs or sitting on benches—there were no benches.

Walkers didn't look their way. Drivers didn't either.

He escorted Hazel to the passenger side and then stepped up behind the wheel. He drove back toward the Dales Inn and thought again—as he had often since they talked—about whether or not he was ready for a serious relationship and even a family. With Hazel he would have one ready-made.

The more he considered that, the more the idea appealed to him, but he could not get past the fear of losing them in some horrible way. If he steered clear of ever having a family outside the one he already belonged to, he would spare himself nearly insurmountable anguish.

Just before they reached the inn, Callum saw a black SUV parked on a side road. The driver was bigger than the person in the gray SUV had been. This was not Carolyn. This was Nate's killer. He had waited there for them, most likely having seen them leave the inn and wisely not followed them as he had before.

Callum sped up, but the killer shot out one of Callum's tires. As he lost control of his vehicle, the right front tire caught on a pothole in the road. Callum could not correct the truck's path and they careened head-on into a tree. Momentarily dazed from the force of the airbag, he shoved the now deflating bag out of the way and saw Hazel doing the same.

"Are you all right?" He searched around for the killer and found him aiming a gun at him through the driver's side window.

He made a roll-the-window-down gesture.

Callum obliged.

"Where is the kid?" the man asked. He wore sunglasses and a beanie hat over longish brown hair. Around six feet tall and of average build, he had the appearance of a regular guy. No tattoos that Callum could see. Clean-shaven. Just as Evie had described to the sketch artist.

"I won't ask you again," the killer said. "Where is the kid?"

Callum had his hand on the door handle. He lifted his other, palm facing the man, more to distract him. "Just calm down."

At the same time that he opened the car door as fast and hard as he could, he karate chopped the man's wrist, knocking his aim off.

The gun fired into the air as the man fell backward.

Callum propelled himself out of the car as the other man rose to his feet. Swinging his foot, Callum kicked the gun from the man's grip, sending it flying into the road. He began to draw his pistol but the other man produced a second gun he had tucked into his boot. Callum ducked behind the open car door in time before bullets struck the side.

Callum fired back when he could, seeing the killer limping from the wound Kerry had inflicted toward the SUV. He shot and missed.

The killer raced off in his SUV, another failed attempt to shoot them.

Looking into the truck, he saw Hazel crouched low, eyes big and dark and round with fear.

"He asked where Evie was," she said.

Neither of them had to ask why. The killer wanted both Hazel and Evie dead. The little girl would be a witness to testify in a trial, if it ever came to that. A familiar wave of dread washed through him. What would become of Hazel and Evie?

Chapter 13

A few days later, Callum thought that Nancy Hersh should be back from her trip to Europe with her husband by now. Callum had told Hazel it would be good for them to be out of Mustang Valley. He was anxious to work more on finding out who shot his father and hopefully proving Ace didn't.

Once again, they stood at Nan's front door and this time she answered. Round faced with short hair dyed blond, she wore visible hearing aids.

"Nancy Hersh?" he asked.

"Yes?" She looked from him to Hazel and back to him. Then she snapped, "I have a No Soliciting sign on my door."

"We're not selling anything. We're trying to track

down someone whose last known whereabouts was at Mustang Valley General Hospital forty years ago."

"My gosh, that's a long time ago."

"Did you go by the name Nan Gelman back then?"

He must want to be sure she was the maternity nurse who worked at the hospital the day of Ace's birth.

"Yes. Nan was a stupid nickname. I don't go by that anymore. People call me by my given name, Nancy. I haven't been Gelman in a very long time. Divorced twice before I met my now-husband."

"So you did work at the hospital?" Hazel asked.

"Yes. I did. I worked on the maternity ward."

"Did you work Christmas Day forty years ago?"

Nancy rolled her eyes irritably. "Yes. In fact, that day forty years ago sticks out like a sore thumb." She told them the year. "For one, a fire broke out that morning and destroyed the nursery records and nurses' station. Also, my rotten supervisor wouldn't give me the day off. I had to work Christmas Eve night and Christmas Day morning. I couldn't stand working for her. She had all the holidays off. Talk about narcissistic. I wanted to give her an award for loving herself more than anyone else I've ever known. She's the reason I left."

Her life had gotten better, at least financially, if she'd just gone on a long European vacation. Hazel wouldn't judge, but many people she had come into contact with who had gotten divorced more than one time had personal issues. She was no expert, though. She only had her few and far between observations.

"Do you remember the babies who were born on Christmas morning?" Callum asked.

"Everybody remembers the babies who are born each Christmas. I remember the ones who were born on New Year's Eve, too." She seemed exceedingly proud of her memory reserves.

"Do you remember a sick baby that day?" Callum asked.

Hazel heard the careful anticipation in his tone. He had high hopes this woman would have something for him.

Her eyebrows lifted. "Oh, yes. I haven't thought of that in such a long time, but the Colton baby boy needed special care. It was quite a memorable time. One of the nurses who worked there gave birth to a healthy baby that same day. Her name was…" The nurse stopped as she searched for a name.

Hazel saw Callum stiffen as though this was a huge piece of information.

"Luella something. I can't remember her last name. But I do remember she left the hospital later that day, the same day she gave birth. I thought that was odd. And the other reason that morning stands out is there was the fire. I'm sure you can imagine the chaos."

"I can," Hazel said. No wonder she remembered that day so vividly after forty years.

"All of the maternity records were destroyed. They were kept in those paper boxes back then." Nancy shook her head and made a *humph* sound.

"I can see why you remember that day so well,"

Callum said. "Are you sure you can't recall Luella's last name?"

Nancy thought for several seconds. "No, I'm sorry, I can't." Then she asked, "Who did you say you were?"

"Callum Colton and Hazel Hart," Callum said.

"Colton. That was one of the babies born that night." She at first seemed thrilled and then not so much. "Why are you asking about that night?"

"We really appreciate all of your help, Nancy." Callum took Hazel's hand and started to turn them away. "Have a good night."

In the rental, Callum seemed edgy and tense. Hazel waited a few seconds.

"What does all that mean?" she asked.

"We have a name," he said. "A first name, but it's more than my family has gotten on Ace's being switched at birth." He turned his head and twisted in the driver's seat as though looking for anything unusual. "We have to be very careful now. If whoever shot my dad knows we came here, we are a target of another killer. I have to get you somewhere safe and work with the police…or not."

As a SEAL? A human weapon? Hazel thought he was taking this to the extreme and she knew why.

"Callum, you don't have to hold yourself responsible for my safety. If the person who shot your father finds out what we learned today, then we are in this together. The same is true for the killer Evie saw. I'm glad you're our bodyguard but if the killer succeeds and Evie and I die, it won't be your fault. It will be the killer's."

He glanced at her sharply, as though he hadn't even realized where his reaction had come from—his penchant to bear all the weight of her well-being.

"I wouldn't want you to feel guilty if anything happens to me, and I'm pretty sure Annabel would have told you the same thing."

His cell phone rang, interrupting what Hazel had hoped would turn into a meaningful conversation.

"Hi, Marlowe," he said.

Hazel waited while he listened.

"All right. We'll stop by now." Then he said to her, "Marlowe asked if I'd stop by the office so she can talk to me."

"About what?"

"She said Payne's assistant found something that might be another clue." He called Kerry next, asking her to meet them at Colton Oil. Then he called Rafe and asked him to gather up everyone in the family and meet them in Marlowe's office.

He was quiet the rest of the way and Hazel wondered if what she had said occupied his mind.

Callum could think of nothing other than what Hazel had said just before Marlowe called. He hadn't even realized his fear was so great that he might not be able to keep Hazel safe. That meant he already felt at least as much for her as he had for Annabel. Even as that thought came, he had a terrible feeling that what he had with Hazel went far deeper. That only terrified him more.

Hazel was right. He couldn't blame himself if someone else killed her. But he could blame himself if he didn't do his job and protect both her and Evie.

Arriving at Colton Oil, he was happy to have other things to keep him focused. They headed right for Marlowe's office.

"That didn't take you long," Marlowe said, standing.

"We weren't far." Callum pulled out one of the desk chairs for Hazel.

She took it and he sat beside her in the other one, facing Marlowe, who dressed like the CEO she was in a black fitted blazer and skirt outfit.

"Dee Walton rushed into my office about an hour ago," Marlowe said.

Dee was his father's assistant. She'd worked part-time since he had gone into the coma, helping Marlowe whenever needed.

"She was in Dad's office getting some files for me. When she dropped them and went to pick them up, she found a pin underneath the air conditioning unit. It's an Arizona State Sun Devils pin, the kind you can get at the university games."

That seemed odd. "Dad isn't an Arizona State Sun Devils fan."

"He does watch football," Marlowe said. "But he has no affiliation with that university."

"Do you think the person who shot him lost it there?" Callum asked.

"Dee thinks that's what happened."

Callum had to agree there was a strong possibility. But how would they ever know?

"This could be the first good clue other than the unhelpful camera footage," Callum said. "Do you agree with Dee?"

"I don't know. I haven't decided. She's been getting into a self-help organization called Affirmation Alliance Group. She can't praise the founder enough. Apparently, Micheline Anderson is gifted at boosting morale and giving healing talks to corporations and individuals. A while back, she asked if we could use them here at Colton Oil, to help people deal with what happened to Dad. She claims they helped her when her husband died last year. I don't know what that group is doing to her state of mind. I hope they're helping her but she may be distracted."

"Do you think they're legit?" Callum asked.

"I'm leery of anything with the word *group* in it. Makes it seem like a cult."

Callum smiled. "Some people go for that sort of thing. The self-help organizations."

Rafe stepped into the office with Ainsley. They both worked at the company, Rafe as CFO and Ainsley as a corporate attorney. Rafe had on an impeccable suit, Ainsley a flowing pantsuit.

"Grayson said he wasn't going to make it," Rafe said. "He also said Asher wouldn't either."

Owner of a first responder agency, Grayson didn't involve himself in Colton Oil matters. Neither did Asher, who was foreman at Rattlesnake Ridge Ranch.

"I'll make sure they know what we discussed today," Marlowe said. "Let's sit over here." She stood and moved everyone to the two sofas that faced each other across a long coffee table.

"Why did you want us all here, Callum?" Rafe asked.

Callum looked behind him and, through the window beside the office door, saw Kerry approaching.

"Ah. Just in time."

Marlowe's assistant, Karen, let the detective in. Her long auburn hair was up in a clip today and her blue eyes found Callum.

"What have you got? Something hot?" she asked, sitting beside him.

Yes, Hazel. Of course, he kept that unbidden thought in his head.

"I found the Mustang Valley General nurse who also gave birth at the hospital the same day as Ace was born," he said. "She quit the same day."

"What? That's huge, Callum," Marlowe said.

"Tell me you have more."

He told her about the nurse who had given birth that Christmas morning and who had left the hospital with the sickly Colton baby rather than her own.

"Her name is Luella," Callum said. "Nancy couldn't recall her last name."

Kerry finished writing on her notepad. "That makes it more difficult."

"But it's a name."

"More than we have so far," Marlowe said.

"Marlowe has some news, as well," Hazel said, joining in the conversation.

Marlowe explained about the pin. Rafe and Ainsley agreed there was a good chance it might have been accidentally left by their father's would-be killer.

"But aren't there Arizona State Sun Devils fans who work here?" Kerry asked, adding her detective insight.

"Yes," Marlowe said. "There are."

"Any one of them could have gone into Payne's office and lost their pin. We will run prints," Kerry said.

"True, but not very many workers other than janitors would have a reason to go in there," Marlowe said.

Not very good janitors, if they'd missed the pin.

"I agree. Finding a connection between the pin and the shooter isn't going to be easy," Callum said. "But it's something to go on."

"Definitely something that needs to be checked out," Kerry said. "Well, thank you for your help, Callum." Kerry nodded to Marlowe. In times like this, Callum was glad to have his family around him.

Back at the inn, Hazel noticed Callum was in a better mood after that meeting. Progress had been made on his father's case but they were still no closer to capturing the killer that Evie had witnessed bashing Nate Blurge over the head. She sensed Callum would be eager to work finding the threat to her and Evie, especially after she'd forced him to face his fear of loving another woman—especially one with a child.

Right now, she just wanted to enjoy a peaceful evening. She missed her daughter terribly. She had already prepared a delicious dinner. Cooking always relaxed her.

She found an action movie that was funny and not too violent and Callum sat beside her. Their talk over dinner had been about what he and his sister had uncovered about their father's shooting. He had also called the hospital to check on Payne. Still no change. Hazel had deliberately avoided any talk about his fears.

Toward the end of the movie, when the hero and heroine acknowledged their mutual attraction, Callum put his arm up and around her.

"Come here," he said.

Warmed that he must be enjoying this quiet evening with just the two of them, she moved closer and rested her head on his muscular chest, in the crook of his arm.

Because she was in her nightgown, only a soft, thin layer separated her bare breasts from his torso. Long, sleeveless and dark green, it covered her well enough and wasn't sexy by any stretch, but she still felt intimate this close to Callum.

Her phone rang. She had been waiting for Evie to

call. Her brother had said they had plans to go to an amusement park for kids.

She sat forward and picked up her phone from the coffee table. "Hi, honey, how was your day?"

"Hi, Mommy," Evie said in a loud, excited voice. "I'm having a blast here. I like Uncle Owen and Aunt Jessica."

"That's great."

"We went to a park today. It had rides. I rode in a teacup with Jessica and a train and a roller coaster!"

"Wow, you did a lot. My brave girl." Hazel knew the roller coaster was a miniature version of those that adults rode.

"And we're having pizza!"

Her brother was going to have corrupted her daughter by the time she went to go get her. "That sounds good."

"I still like your food, Mommy. You're the best cook ever."

"Aw, thanks Evie."

"When are you coming to get me?"

Hazel wished she could say *right now, right this minute*. "I don't know yet. I'll call you as soon as I do, okay?"

"Okay." Evie's tone dimmed considerably.

Hazel felt both loved by her daughter and sad, which put a damper on her mood.

"What are you doing right now?" Evie asked.

"I was watching a movie with Callum."

"What movie?"

"None that you would like. An adult movie."

"Can we watch *Brave* when I get home?"

"Of course." She heard Owen say in the background that they had that movie there. Hazel was going to start to get jealous.

"Can I talk to Cal-em?" Evie asked.

Hazel was surprised by the request. Why did she want to talk to Callum?

"Sure." She put the phone on speaker—she wasn't about to miss a single second of this. "Evie wants to say hi," she said to Callum.

"Hi, Cal-em."

"Hi, Evie. You having fun?" He sounded as though he was a good sport but Hazel wondered if this would be difficult for him.

"Yes! I like my uncle and aunt's house. They're fun."

"That's good."

"Did you catch the bad guy yet?" she asked.

"I'm not a policeman. Kerry is the one who will catch him," Callum said.

"Did Mommy tell you I'm gonna be a police girl when I grow up?"

"No, she didn't. Why do you want to do that?"

"So I can get a badge and catch bad people," she said. "Why didn't you be a policeman?"

Callum looked at Hazel with a grin. Evie was full of questions today.

"I suppose I wanted to protect people instead of catch the ones who hurt them."

A few seconds passed as Evie absorbed that. "I want to protect people, too. That's what Kerry does."

"Yes, she's one of the good guys."

"She's a girl."

Callum chuckled. "Yes, she is."

A few more seconds passed and Hazel thought her daughter had run out of steam at last.

"Cal-em?"

"Yes?"

"Are you going to come with Mommy to pick me up?"

Callum glanced at Hazel. When the time came to go get Evie, all the danger would have passed. What would Callum do? Would he run?

"Of course, I'll be there," he said.

Hazel felt a surge of warmth and hope. Maybe there was a chance for them, after all.

Did she want that? It didn't take much thinking to know what her heart desired. Yes, she did. She wanted a chance to be a couple with him, maybe more.

"Are you going to come live with us?" Evie asked.

"I already have a place to live."

He lived in a mansion.

"But you like Mommy, don't you?"

"Yes, I do like her very much."

"And you like me?" she asked in a singsong voice.

"Yes, even more."

Evie laughed, a lighthearted giggle. "Nuh-uh. You like Mommy more."

Callum chuckled again, seeming to really enjoy the banter with the girl.

"I see you with her," Evie said. "You like her a lot."

"I said I did."

"Then you should come live with us, then."

Evie was so fond of him. Hazel would worry about her state of mind if he left them, but Evie was working her kid-charmed magic on him.

"Pizza's here," Hazel heard Owen say in the background.

"You better go get pizza while it's hot," Callum said.

"Okay. See you soon."

"See you soon."

Evie must have disconnected herself. Owen or Jessica didn't come back on. Hazel leaned back against the sofa with a sigh.

"I miss her so much," she said.

Callum put his arm back around her. "She is something else. Adorable."

She tipped her head up and over to see him. "Yes, she's a heart melter."

He smiled softly, meeting her eyes.

"She likes you a lot," Hazel said.

"How does a man who leaves a pregnant woman create such a gem?" he asked.

"That's easy. She got most of her good traits from me." Hazel smiled up teasingly.

"I'd say."

And there they went again, falling into this sexual energy. They looked into each other's eyes, which ended with him lowering his mouth to hers. Basking in the aftermath of his affectionate words, she grew hot all over.

She touched his face as the kiss deepened. When that didn't satisfy her raging desire, she climbed onto him.

"Uh." He grunted and then slid his hands to her rear to move her over his jean-clad erection.

She was lost at that point. All that mattered was him and how he made her feel.

He pulled up the hem of her long nightgown. She kept kissing him as his hands traveled slowly up her thighs to her bare butt.

Pulling back from the kiss, he met her eyes.

She smiled from pleasure in his heated response. Lifting his T-shirt to get it out of the way, she unbuttoned his jeans and then unzipped them as much as she could. He helped her by raising his hips, which incited her more because of the pressure. He pushed his jeans and underwear down.

Hazel resumed kissing him and moved back on top of him. His hands returned to her rear and their breathing became more ragged. She ran her hands along his hard chest, brushing her thumbs over his stiff nipples.

Callum lifted her nightgown and she raised her hands so he could take it off. He let it fall onto the sofa beside them. Then he gripped the back of her head and pressed an urgent kiss to her lips. She reciprocated with equal verve, moving over his erection.

With a gruff sound, he set her down over him. She was so wet and ready for him. Shivers of sensation numbed her to all else. She had to stay still for a moment, lest the pleasure end too soon.

She planted a kiss on his mouth. "I've never felt like this before." Her voice came out as a breathless whisper.

"Neither have I," he answered in kind.

That he'd confessed such a thing stimulated her passion even more. She kissed him long and deep, needing to soak every part of him into her.

He pumped his hips. Evidently his patience had run out. Bracing her hands on his shoulders, she did the same in rhythm with him. And just a few strokes later she came with such intensity she cried out.

He groaned his own release and she continued to move on him, not wanting this to end.

At last she put her forehead against his. He moved until he found her mouth for a gentle kiss. The tender, sweet action captured her heart. She was beyond backing off. She could not without suffering pain. Losing Callum would be the biggest heartbreak of her life.

Chapter 14

The next day, Callum stood in front of the bathroom mirror and admitted to himself that he would have difficulty leaving Hazel. But he would have more difficulty losing her permanently. At a loss for what to do, how to preserve himself if the worst happened, he fell into silent contemplation. Hazel had studied him more than once but never confronted him. That made him fall in love with her even more. She gave him the space he needed without judging.

Wait...

Had he just thought that he had fallen in love with her?

He finished getting into his biker disguise, wig and glasses in place. He left the bathroom to find

Hazel waiting, way too sexy for his confused state. He would rather take all her clothes off and stay home.

"You ready?" They were headed to Joe's Bar to conduct another stakeout.

Her white-toothed smile and animated manner warmed a nonsexual part of him. This was Hazel. Positive. Loving. Strong in so many ways.

A mother...

"Yes."

He offered his hand, more of an obligatory gesture. He was so out of sorts.

She didn't take it. Instead, she studied him before saying, "Last night was beautiful."

Beautiful.

He had other words come to mind. Scorching hot. Heart-wrenching, in a really good way.

"I am happy with just that, Callum," she said. "Don't feel pressured. I know you have been through a lot. I'll be all right no matter what happens. Evie will be, too, because she has me."

The truth of what she said penetrated deep into him. Hazel would never push him. She wanted him for who he was and nothing less. She cared about him, his happiness above all else. He wanted to give that to her, as well. All of him. But he still felt so broken. So injured. A woman like her deserved the whole man.

He slid his hand behind her head, gently, then stepped close. Kissing her, he hoped she understood the unspoken message, how amazing and charitable she was.

When he drew back she put her forefinger over

his lips as though sealing the kiss. "Let's go catch that bad guy."

"Hazel..."

"Shh." She lowered her hand. "None of that now. Let's go."

He took a moment to enjoy how beautiful she was and how sexy in that biker-woman disguise. "I must be a fool."

She put her pointer finger on his upper chest and ran it down to the waist of his pants. Then her striking eyes looked up at him. "You could never be a fool, Callum Colton. You just need to let go of past pain. I only hope I'm still in your life when you do."

She looked into his eyes, angling her head and assessing him. After she must have learned what she needed to from peering into his eyes, she turned and headed for the suite's entrance.

Rather than take a hired car, Callum called a cab. That would be less conspicuous. On the way, Callum phoned Kerry to let her know about their visit. She wasn't happy with their planning something like that on their own and on such short notice, but she said she'd assemble a team to wait in unmarked cars in the parking lot. She'd also send a plainclothes cop inside in case anything went wrong.

A short drive later, they reached the bar. Callum made sure no one saw them as they left the cab.

He guided Hazel into Joe's. After being seated they settled in to have an evening together, covertly surveying everyone there.

It was much the same as the last time they were there. Dim and dirty.

And the same biker crowd was at the pool table.

All appeared calm, until Callum noticed a red-headed waitress who kept looking behind her and all around the bar.

"Did you see that redhead last time we were here?" he asked Hazel.

She looked around the bar and zeroed in on the other woman. "No."

Hazel moved closer to him. "Might as well look the part."

"Careful."

"Of what?" She leaned in, her breast pressing against his side.

"Of more." He could have elaborated but he didn't.

"You should give in. You have no control over this. I realized that after last night."

She was sure being bold. Yes, last night had been earth-shattering. He couldn't face that right now.

"Let's get rid of this killer and then deal with that, okay?"

She smiled wide and bright. "Okay." Then she turned to survey the bar, covertly watching the red-head serve beers to a table of raucous men.

"She's wearing a wedding ring," Callum said. He looked at the other female workers. There were only two and neither wore a ring. If the killer had murdered Nate Blurge for flirting with his wife, he might have shown up tonight to keep an eye on her.

"The woman who served us last time didn't have one," Hazel said.

"And the redhead wasn't working that night, so if she is his wife, the killer probably wasn't here."

"Nope." She looked around the bar and he saw her stop short when she spotted a table with a lone man sitting there.

He was the same height and build as the man who kept showing up at the inn and following them and shooting at them. He had no hat on and no sunglasses. In a holey pair of faded jeans and a black *Deadwood* T-shirt, he had a day or two's worth of facial stubble. His longish brown hair convinced Callum he was their man.

"He's watching the redhead," Hazel said.

Yes, he was. And very intently. The killer's face turned stormy, his brows lowered. He had all the mannerisms of an insanely jealous man, a power tripper. He looked the type to need absolute control over his woman. He was so involved with policing the redhead that he didn't notice Callum and Hazel watching him.

Callum looked back at the waitress and saw her smiling at one of the men drinking at a table. The man didn't seem drunk. He was clean-cut and dressed in dark jeans with no holes in them and a nice polo. Callum watched him after the redhead left the table. He wasn't drinking fast and when the others ordered another round, he declined. He made the redhead smile and this time laugh as he talked with her.

"Oh boy," Hazel said.

Callum looked over at the killer. He had gotten up and marched across the bar toward the man at the table.

Standing up, Callum heard the killer say in a loud, angry tone, "Why are you flirting with my wife?"

Looking startled, the man looked up. "I didn't know she was married."

"She's wearing a ring, you idiot!"

"I didn't look, sorry, man. All I did was thank her for the beer and tell her she was too pretty to be working in a place like this."

"Why did she laugh like you said something funny?"

The other man stood. "Dude, calm down. Nothing happened. Just casual talk. You should be flattered I think you have a beautiful wife."

A woman who deserved better than a killer as a husband. Callum watched that man shove the other.

"Do you always hit on other men's wives?"

"Hey. What's your problem?" The man shoved him back.

The killer took a swing, hitting the other man. Callum stalked to them, planting his hand on the murderer's chest and getting between them.

"That's enough." Callum pushed the killer back, forcing him to step farther away from him and the clean-cut man.

The man behind him tried to get around Callum to go after the killer. Callum lost some balance and the killer took a swing at him and clipped his jaw. Callum's glasses went flying. The man behind him had grabbed hold of his wig, pulling it off his head. The man had meant to pull him out of the way but the wig stopped him.

Callum gave him a shove and growled, "Back off!"

"You!" the killer snarled, recognizing Callum.

Callum ducked as the killer made another swing at him and the punch caught the man behind him. Callum swiped his opponent's leg out from under him, sending him down. But the killer lunged for him, plowing into him and driving them both back into the table of drinking men. Callum landed on his back, spilling beer glasses and scattering the seated men.

Using his feet, Callum kicked the killer, sending him flying backward and sliding on his back through the broken and spilled glasses of beer. He bumped into another table.

Going toward him, he saw the killer get to his feet and look around, finding Hazel standing near their table. The other man sprinted toward her, causing an instant flash of fear in Callum.

He ran to Hazel as the killer drew a pistol and she pivoted and started to head for the exit. But the killer was on her too fast. He grabbed her, spun her around and put the pistol to her temple.

Callum stopped short, just a couple of feet from them. He looked at Hazel's terrified eyes. She must be thinking of her daughter. Callum had failed her.

He stood frozen for a few seconds, before anger took over. No way would he lose another woman like this!

With a lightning-fast gesture, he knocked the gun

upward. It went off but the bullet shot toward the ceiling. Callum kicked the man and sent him back and away from Hazel. As Kerry and other officers, including the plainclothes cop, burst in, Hazel ran to the bar and huddled with some other people, and Callum drew his own gun and aimed it at the killer's head.

"I've got you now," Callum said to the man on the floor. Finally.

Kerry approached.

"That's him," Callum said. "That's the man Evie saw hit Nate Blurge over the head."

Kerry glanced at him sharply. "You're certain?"

"As certain as I can be. He's the same build and his hair is the same."

She nodded to two officers, who knelt down and searched the man, procuring a driver's license and handing it to Kerry.

"Billy Jansen," she said. "Run this by Motor Vehicle."

One of the officers left with the license.

Moments later the officer returned with the license and announced the plate number was a match.

"Take him to the station," Kerry said to the other officer.

The officer helped Billy to his feet and cuffed him, reading him his rights.

"The redhead over there is his wife," Callum said, pointing to the woman next to Hazel who watched Billy with no small amount of apprehension.

"We'll need to talk to her."

"I'll tell her."

Callum walked over to Hazel and the redhead.

"Are you all right?" he asked Hazel.

"Yes, thanks to you." She rose up on her toes and kissed him, quick and grateful.

"You're welcome." Nothing felt better than that.

Facing the redhead, he said, "The police are going to want to talk to you."

"Why? They're doing me a favor taking him away."

"You're his wife. You can provide information they'll need to prosecute him and testify against him if you want to."

"How long will he be in jail?"

She was obviously worried he'd get out and come after her.

"If he gets convicted of murder, he'll be in prison for the rest of his life. What's your name?"

"Tina Jansen."

"What can you tell police about Nate Blurge's murder?"

"Plenty. He flirted with me the same way that nice man tonight did and ended up dead. Billy wasn't home when Nate was killed and Billy bragged about getting rid of him. He even threatened me that he'd kill every man I flirted with."

"Your testimony will only help. I can assure you he'll be put away for a long time." Callum couldn't believe that some killers talked about what they had done.

Tina smiled big. "Good riddance. I can finally divorce him without worrying he'll kill me, too."

Callum didn't doubt that. He was glad the man would be off the streets, but he still had one more problem to take care of before he could be assured of Hazel's safety.

Most of the police had gone and the bar had returned to its usual business. Hazel couldn't wait to get out of her disguise. She went to the bathroom before she and Callum would go home. Finishing up, she washed her hands at the sink. They could retrieve Evie soon. When she lifted her head, she saw Carolyn's reflection in the mirror and she had a gun.

Seriously? Hazel's disbelief buffered the slight gasp of shock and fear.

The same night? "How did you know we were here?"

"Easy. I knew you were looking for that Blurge man's killer and Patsy told me you were going to be here one of these nights."

Damn that assistant.

"If you don't come quietly, I'll shoot you. It's what I've dreamed of doing ever since you left my restaurant. I knew I could never make it without a chef like you and I knew I'd have a hard time replacing you."

"Carolyn, you don't have to do this. I told you I was sorry. I never meant for any of that to happen."

"It's too late for all of that. I thought I could forgive you but I can't. Now get moving."

Hazel hesitated. If she went with this crazy woman, she would probably end up dead before morning. She had to find a way to alert Callum.

Callum.

What would this do to him? And what about Evie?

More determined than ever, Hazel started toward the bathroom exit. Carolyn jabbed her gun against Hazel's ribs, concealing the gun with the oversized sweatshirt she wore.

Would anyone find an oversized sweatshirt odd? Arizona was hot, but it was early spring and nighttime, when it got colder.

Outside the bathroom, Hazel stalled. Just as she suspected, Callum stood where he could see the bathroom. And he spotted her right away.

"Get going!" Carolyn jabbed her and forced her to hurry to the back door, which had been propped open to allow airflow.

They passed the kitchen entrance, where heat poured out through the narrow doorway along with the sounds of frying food and workers having a lighthearted night.

Hazel dared not look back to see where Callum was. Carolyn forced her through the back door, and to Hazel's horror, she had her SUV parked right outside and the driver's side door was open. Carolyn had planned to make Hazel drive, presumably with a gun pointed at her in case she tried to escape or attract attention.

Did a dive bar like this have cameras? Not likely.

Hazel knew she had to do something. She could not get in that vehicle before Callum caught up to them.

Relying—desperately—on what she had heard about self-defense, she dropped all her weight straight down. Carolyn wasn't a big woman. Hazel felt her former boss stumble and rake at her clothes, to no avail. She stepped back to maintain her balance. It was enough for Hazel to scramble away, looking for cover.

She didn't have to panic long. Callum emerged from the back door, smacking Carolyn's head with the butt of his pistol, and she fell like a rag doll. He kicked her gun away and rushed over to Hazel.

"Are you all right?" He was breathless and his eyes were wild with fear.

She just grabbed his face with both hands and kissed him hard once. "Yes. I am, Callum. I love you." She kissed him hard again and then stopped herself.

What had she said? The words had tumbled out.

Heat hardened his eyes from frantic concern. Was the tension sexual—or maybe loving? But it appeared only for an instant.

"Go inside and get the police," he said.

She did as he asked. But as she ran into the bar and to the front, the glow of warmth she had seen in him crept into her in a different way. He'd caught the feeling and shut it off.

He wasn't ready for this, for her to have blurted out words of love.

Outside, she found the officers and told them about Carolyn. They instructed her to wait. She'd have to give a statement and so would Callum.

She would rather call a cab and go get Evie, go home and forget any of this ever happened. She needed Evie more than ever. But she'd have to wait.

Chapter 15

Callum woke late the next morning. Having to give statements on two criminal incidents had taken time. He reached over to feel for Hazel and then remembered she had insisted on sleeping in her own room. He'd had a bad feeling about that the previous night, but the hour had been so late and both of them so tired he hadn't argued.

Now, with a clear head, he realized all of the adrenaline and his baggage with Annabel had taken their toll.

Hoping against hope, he flung the covers off and went across the hall. The room was immaculate. No trace of Hazel. The bed was made and all her things, and Evie's, were gone.

He ran his hand through his hair. He needed his sister.

After quickly showering, he raced to Marlowe's office, pacing outside until the worker she had a meeting with left. Then he went inside and closed the door.

"I heard you captured two criminals in one night. Nice going, brother."

"I need to tell you something." He could not believe he was going to do this.

He paced her office, one side to the other, three times.

"Okay, you're worrying me," Marlowe said.

He stopped and put his hands on the back of one of the chairs facing her desk and looked at her, still struggling with how to begin.

She angled her head. "This whole…" she twirled her pen a few times "…weak man thing isn't the twin I grew up with."

Callum lowered his head with a sigh. She had a way of reaching him he could never explain to anyone. He lifted his head. "There's something I haven't told almost anyone."

Marlowe lifted her eyebrows. "Go on. Don't stop now."

She knew him so well. He would have stopped, in this fragile state. Pushing off the chair, he straightened. "Annabel and I didn't break up."

Marlowe didn't move or blink. She just waited.

"She died."

His sister's mouth formed an O on an indrawn breath. "You lied?"

"I'm sorry." He opened his arms. "I'm so sorry."

"Stop being so weak. What happened?" she demanded.

Lowering his arms and taking a chair, he explained everything, the witness and Annabel's pregnancy—and her death.

"We knew all of that, Callum. What *happened*?"

"I was protecting a witness and was in court a lot. The drug cartel must have had me followed and the leader sent someone to assassinate her. I wasn't there to protect her."

Marlowe took several seconds to absorb that and, Callum knew, piece together what he hadn't said.

"Oh, Cal." She shook her head gently, full of empathy. And then she grew stern. "And you didn't tell *me*?"

"I didn't tell anyone. I couldn't." He had no way of explaining.

As it turned out, he didn't have to. His sister knew him like no other. "You blamed yourself but because you met Hazel, you can face it now."

Well, that he hadn't expected. His sister knew how to get to the point, but that was…he would have thought harsh but he checked himself. Her honesty, like Hazel's, showed him not only the brutality of the truth but also the healing power of facing it.

"Tell you what." Marlowe leaned back in her big leather executive chair. "I'll tell the family, and you go get this woman who's done you so much good."

Callum felt his insides twist with warning. "What? No. It's not like that."

Marlowe picked up a pen from the desk and dropped it in exasperation. "It's not? Look at you. Listen to yourself. You just told me that meeting Hazel has brought you here, confessing something huge that you kept from your own family."

He hadn't thought how his inability to deal with Annabel's death would affect his siblings. He hadn't cared about his parents all that much. They were always too involved with Colton Oil. And other than with Marlowe, he wasn't the type of brother to bleed out his soul to everyone. But Marlowe...

"I should have told you," he said. "You're right." He ran his fingers through his hair, disconcerted.

"Stop," Marlowe said. "Just stop."

He looked at her, not sure of her meaning.

"You should have told me, but I understand why you didn't. I know you like you know me. We are tough emotionally, and smart and strong. But we can be stubborn, Cal."

"I know, but—"

"What I want you to hear from me—and you better listen—is you have met a beautiful and wonderful woman who won't put up with your baggage if you can't handle it."

Nothing like putting it bluntly. He also liked the handling connotation. Baggage. Handles.

He laughed, deeply and from his core. "Marlowe, I love you."

"Go get that girl, you fool." She smiled and

laughed softly in return. "There's no escaping it. Take it from one who knows."

She'd gotten involved with Bowie Robertson, the president of Robertson Renewable Energy Company, Colton Oil's rival. She'd gotten pregnant and ended up falling in love. Callum still couldn't tell she was pregnant. She looked great.

Resigned to the fact that she was probably right, he stood from the chair.

"Hey," Marlowe said.

He met her teasing eyes.

"Do you love her?"

He recalled Hazel blurting she loved him and how that had made him feel. Confused. Scared. Weak, as his sister would say.

"Yes."

Both let down by Callum's brusque attitude and exceedingly excited to see Evie again, Hazel walked up to her brother's house. Owen opened the door before she got there and Evie bounded out.

"Mommy!"

Immense joy burst in Hazel. She crouched as Evie ran to her and took her into her arms. "Hi, Evie. I missed you so much."

"I missed you, too, Mommy."

Hazel kissed her cheek several times, making Evie laugh. Then she stood up.

Evie looked toward the street. "Where's Cal-em?"

"He couldn't make it." Seeing Evie's crestfallen face, Hazel felt a pang of guilt for not bringing Callum with her. She'd figured a clean break would be best for her daughter.

"But he said he would."

"I know, honey." She took her daughter's hand and walked to her brother.

"She's a great kid. Whatever you're doing, keep doing it."

She hugged Owen. "Where's Jessica?"

"She went to work. She said to tell you hello and thanks for convincing her to have kids. I'd like to thank you, too."

Hazel smiled, loving Evie's effect on them. "I didn't know you wanted them."

"I wasn't sure until now." He messed up the top of Evie's hair, which she wore down today. "You come back anytime, okay?"

"Okay!"

"Thank you so much, Owen. I owe you big for watching her."

"I'm just glad you caught that killer. We were scared for you. And your ex-boss." He shook his head with raised eyebrows. "That's so wild."

"Yeah. I still can't believe it. She was always so friendly."

"I guess everybody has their breaking point."

Even if Hazel ran into hard times like that, she didn't think she would ever break to the point of attempted murder. "I think I'd have to be on my deathbed before I broke."

"Yes, and normal people wouldn't murder anybody."

"No." She looked down at Evie. "Well, what do you think, kiddo? Should we go home?"

"Okay. Will Cal-em be there?"

"I don't think so."

Her brother eyed her in question. "I thought you two had something going."

She had to be careful what she said in front of Evie. She couldn't be sure what Callum would do, now that she was safe.

"It's still too early to tell."

"That's not how it looked to me," Owen said. "I've never seen you glow like you did with him nearby."

She'd been glowing? She had not been aware of that.

"Why didn't he come with you today?" Owen asked.

"I left early. I didn't wake him," she said neutrally. "We better get going. I've got a lot of meals to cook."

"Don't let a good man go because of what Ed did to you," Owen said. "And don't hold it against Callum for being rich. He isn't the same as Ed."

"I know, Owen." She might as well tell him all of it, Evie, too. "He has issues of his own. His pregnant girlfriend died in an accident. A drug dealer did it to get revenge on Callum for him protecting a witness during his trial. He hasn't gotten over her yet."

"All he needs is someone like you to know he has a soft place to land."

She was a soft place to land? Not if being with Evie all the time made him think of the baby he had lost. And not if he held back with Hazel and never let his feelings grow with her. She wanted more than that and Evie deserved more than that.

When Hazel arrived back at her little apartment above the bakery, she did not expect to see Callum's rental parked in the back.

"Cal-em's here!" Evie exclaimed.

Hazel parked and walked around to get Evie out of her car seat. She fidgeted and swung her tiny feet, anxious to get out of the SUV. Since she had been riding in Callum's vehicles, the Mercedes' mirror had been repaired.

She freed Evie, who climbed out of the SUV and ran toward the stairs. Hazel followed, wondering why Callum was here. She saw him get out of the truck as they approached. Evie veered away from the stairs.

"Evie!" Callum crouched and wrapped his arms around her as she crashed into him.

"You said you were gonna come get me," Evie said, small arms looping around his neck as she leaned back to look at his face.

"I'm sorry. That's why I'm here now." He looked at Hazel.

She saw pure adoration for Evie's sweet charm.

"And I also came to have a word with your mother."

Evie glanced back at Hazel.

"Let's go inside." Hazel walked to the stairs and Callum carried Evie up them. Inside, she felt she no longer belonged in this tiny place. She still wasn't sure she would be comfortable living in a mansion with all of Callum's family, or if she would get used to having so much money—that was, if he did love her.

He put Evie down and told her to go find them a good movie. She trotted to the living room.

Hazel faced Callum, prepared for anything. He was gentleman enough to make sure he talked to her personally about any decisions he had made.

He took her hands in his. "This last month with you has been more than eye-opening, Hazel."

"For me, as well."

"First I want to start off by saying I am nothing like Evie's father. I don't run from difficult situations or circumstances."

"I know that about you." He would face her and break things off ethically and with integrity.

"I'm rich like he was, probably richer, because of my family."

She nodded, lowering her eyes.

"But I have never lied to you, nor will I ever."

She returned her gaze to him. This was beginning to sound like he had no intention of breaking things off between them. Hope flared and her heart began to pound with responding emotion.

"You helped me through dealing with Annabel's death. And talking to my sister today made me realize that even though it's only been a month, I've fallen in love with you."

She couldn't believe her ears.

"That's why..." He got down on one knee and then let go of her hands to dig into his pocket.

No way. He wasn't...

He pulled out a ring box. "Now, I don't want you to feel rushed." He looked up at her and opened the box to reveal a sapphire and diamond ring. The sapphires were about a karat between them and surrounded by smaller diamonds. A man with his money could have gotten her something gaudy and blatantly expensive. But he knew her. He knew she wouldn't have appreciated anything like that.

"You pick the date, but will you marry me?"

Tears stung her eyes. This was the happiest day of her life! "When did you…"

"I stopped at the jewelry store on the way here. I knew you were going to get Evie so I had plenty of time. I guessed on the size."

She stared at the ring, loving it enormously.

"You haven't answered my question," he said.

She glanced at Evie, who was oblivious to this monumental moment. Hazel didn't have to worry she wouldn't approve. She was already treating Callum like her stepfather.

Then she looked at Callum. "Yes, I will marry you. I don't care when. It can be tomorrow or next spring. I'll still want to marry you as much as I do right now, because I have fallen in love with you, too."

Smiling, he stood and removed the ring from the box. She offered her hand and he slipped it on her finger. It fit perfectly.

Chapter 16

Marlowe had arranged for a family gathering at the mansion to allow Hazel to get to know everyone better. Over the last few days, he had relished in living with Hazel and Evie as a family. They had decided to stay at the inn a while longer to enjoy some downtime. Callum thought a get-together would be a perfect opportunity to show Hazel his home and let her decide if it was somewhere she wanted to live. They didn't have to live in the mansion. They could build something on the ranch. It was Sunday afternoon on a sunny, clear day.

"You all live here?" Hazel asked when the sprawling mansion appeared. Made of rock and wood to match the rugged landscape and the Mustang Valley Mountains in the distance, the multiple gables of the roofline and three stories of windows and balconies gave evidence to its size.

"Yes. My mom and dad live on the first floor in one wing. There are guest quarters in the other wing. Ace, Grayson and Ainsley have the three wings on the second floor, and Asher, Marlowe and I have the third floor wings. Then there are several spaces we share, like the living areas and the library."

He parked and got out, waiting for Hazel to get Evie out of the back. She had slept the whole way there. Now she groggily walked beside Hazel to the entrance. There were other cars here, but most were likely in the huge garage.

Inside the grand entry, Hazel took in the luxurious, floor-to-ceiling windows and exposed beam ceiling of the open living room. Callum saw most everyone was already here. The only ones missing were Grayson and Asher.

"Callum." Marlowe came to greet them, leaving Bowie standing with a glass of wine near the rock pillars at the entrance of the large dining room.

Kerry was there with Rafe, seated on the sofa with Ainsley.

"I sent someone to get Grayson and Asher. They should be here soon." She turned to Hazel. "So happy to see you. Looks like I talked some sense into my brother after all."

"Thanks for that." Hazel showed her the ring.

"Oh, that's beautiful!" Marlowe gaped at Callum. "Everybody, Callum is getting married!" She held Hazel's hand out for all to see.

"He's gonna be my new daddy," Evie said. Then, seeing the huge television, she meandered over. Ainsley changed the channel to a kid friendly show.

Hazel mouthed, *Thank you.*

Just then Grayson and Asher entered. All the siblings were together, a few of them attached to significant others.

Callum rarely saw Grayson. He doubted any of the others did, either.

"This is Hazel, Callum's fiancée." Marlowe introduced her to the two. "And her daughter, Evie."

Grayson reached over and shook her hand. "Fianceé?"

"Hey, it's about time."

"And that is Asher," Marlowe said. "He's Rattlesnake Ridge Ranch's foreman and a bit of a lone wolf."

"A pleasure to meet you both. You look like a real cowboy, Asher," Hazel said. "With the longish hair and that face, you must make all the women swoon."

Grayson chuckled. "He's a lone wolf. He doesn't date."

Asher shook his head. "Thank you for the compliment, Hazel, and it's nice to meet you, too. Callum needs a good woman in his life. And a good daughter!"

"Thanks. What do you do, Grayson?"

"I run a first responder management agency."

"That sounds exciting. Do you like rescuing people?"

"He likes the adrenaline rush," Callum said.

"Yes," Grayson said to Hazel, "Helping people is the most rewarding part." Then he turned a disgruntled look to Callum.

"I've been trying to get a hold of both of you to update you on the whole situation with Dad," Marlowe said.

She hadn't told them yet?

"We found the woman who gave birth on the Christmas morning the babies were switched." Callum explained about the fire and the woman who'd left that same day with what everyone thought was her baby but must have been their biological brother.

"Her name is Luella. We don't have a last name yet," Marlowe said.

"Well, that's good news, I mean that you have at least a first name. Is she the one who switched Ace with our biological brother?" Asher asked.

"Yes, it is possible," Callum said.

"What kind of sicko does that?" Asher asked. "We need to catch her and find out, brother. Is he still alive?"

"I want to help," Grayson said. "What can I do?"

Callum found his brother's concern odd. He believed that Grayson did like helping people but this was different. "You haven't even gone to see Dad in the hospital. Why are you so gung-ho now to step up? You don't even hang out with your family. It's like putting a house fire out to get you to come to any of these."

"Somebody switched our oldest brother. That nurse has to pay. We have to get justice for Ace. He may not be our blood brother but he's still our sibling."

"Isn't that the truth," Ainsley said.

"We can't stop until we do find this Luella and bring her to justice," Rafe said from the sofa.

"I just want to know why you care all of a sudden," Callum said. The fact that he wasn't close to his brothers and sisters and never went to see their dad in the hospital didn't support Grayson's assertions.

"My relationship was always complicated with Dad. I'm sure you've had your ups and downs with him. I haven't resolved anything with him. I'm not sure he'd want to see me."

"Dad's in a coma. You should go for yourself, not him."

Grayson didn't respond right away. "It's not that simple, Callum."

"It can be. Just go see him. Talk to him. He might be in a coma but he can still hear."

"That's true," Marlowe said. "His brain will still hear you."

"You'd side with Callum anyway," Grayson said. "You're his twin."

Marlowe put her hands up. "I think it would be good for you to go see him. It has nothing to do with agreeing with Cal."

"Anyway, the real problem here is finding whoever switched Ace," Grayson said. "I want to find our real brother. He's out there somewhere and probably has no idea where he really came from."

"I feel so bad for Ace," Ainsley said. "Why isn't he here?"

"He's laying low for now," Callum said. "Until we can find out who shot Dad."

"Yeah, but he's all alone," Ainsley said. "And what he must be going through, dealing with the discovery that he isn't a Colton by blood. Does he think we all consider him an outsider?"

"I don't think so," Callum said. "At least, not everyone."

"Dad?" Marlowe put in. "Kicking him out of Colton Oil?"

"It's not enough to make Ace try to kill him," Grayson said.

"I think all of us want to believe that," Ainsley said.

"Yeah," Rafe said.

"Of course," Asher said. He walked into the kitchen, lone wolf that he was.

"Let's start with finding Luella," Callum said.

"Hey," Marlowe said. "Let's turn this into a celebration for Callum and Hazel—and Evie, too."

"Hear, hear." Ainsley lifted her glass.

Callum turned to Hazel and slipped his arm around her waist. "Hear, hear, for sure."

The siblings began talking of other things, leaving Callum and Hazel with a moment to themselves.

"Let me show you my wing," Callum said. "You can tell me what you think."

He took her to the third level. It took some time to get there, the home was so large. Then he arrived at a door and opened it. She stepped inside an expansive seating area with a high ceiling, a fireplace and a balcony. There was a bar, as well, and a dining table and kitchenette. That she didn't like. He showed her the master suite. It was magnificent, with a huge bathroom. No room for Evie.

"It doesn't seem suitable for a family," she said.

"I thought the same. I didn't expect you to want to live here. We can build a house here on the ranch or somewhere else."

She would probably like his family but living so close to them seemed too much for her. She preferred to have her privacy. They could come see his family as often as he liked.

"I'm not sure I want to wait that long to move into a house," she said.

"All right." He smiled. "We'll look somewhere in town." He kissed her and, as always, their chemistry heated. With a bed so close, taking this further was tempting, but with his siblings and her daughter downstairs, they should be getting back.

Hazel drew away and just looked at Callum, into his loving and incredible blue eyes. She had to be one of the luckiest women in the world.

Hazel and Callum opted for staying at the Dales Inn until they could find a house. They were headed there now, with Callum driving. But then she noticed he wasn't heading in the direction of town.

"Where are we going?"

"I have a surprise for you," he said with a wily grin.

"Callum Colton, what are you up to?"

"Yeah. Whatcha up to?" Evie asked from the back seat.

"You'll see. If I tell you it will ruin the surprise." He drove into a rural area outside Mustang Valley city limits, into an affluent neighborhood with large homes but not mansions. The houses were all stone with big windows and each measured about five thousand square feet.

She had a pretty good idea what his surprise was going to be. She turned to him.

"If you don't like it, we can look for another one," Callum said, having read her glance.

What was there not to like?

He pulled to a stop in front of a beautiful gray stone house with white trim. There was a veranda next to the front portico and a turret on the other side.

"My family already owns this house," Callum said. "It's technically a Colton family property but my mom, as my dad's representative, said she could transfer the title to us once we're married."

"It's beautiful." She helped Evie out of the truck and walked toward the front entrance. Inside, a two-story foyer soared above a spiral staircase going to the second level. The formal living room to the left had a fireplace and was open to the dining room, where double doors led to the veranda. A groin-vaulted ceiling over a short hallway opened to the living room and kitchen area.

The kitchen.

It was obviously professional grade, but without an overwhelming amount of stainless steel, with white walls and recessed lighting. The perimeter cabinets were white and the countertops soft green granite. The kitchen island drew her like a magnet. It had a green hood with a pan holder where several pots and pans already hung. There was a five-burner stove set in dark brown and tan granite that had a counter-mounted pot filler, which allowed a cook to fill big pots with water. The stainless steel refrigerator was twice the size of the one in her apartment. There were two ovens and a microwave was mounted into a cabinet. It was a dream kitchen.

"It was designed for hired cooks to entertain guests who stay here," Callum said.

Overwhelmed, Hazel turned in a circle and just admired it. She felt like she was in a dream. "I don't need to see the rest of the house."

"Can I pick out my room?" Evie asked.

Callum chuckled. "Sure." He showed them two master suites and two other bedrooms on the second level. There was also a theater room. He took them to a room done in pale blue, light gray and white that had a built-in oversized bunk bed, the top more like a mini balcony. There was a seating area, built-in bookshelf and an antique trunk.

"Wow!" Evie ran to the bunk bed and climbed up the white ladder to her tower, peering down at them with a big smile.

"There's toys in the trunk," Callum said. "Marlowe had it filled."

"Come on," he said to Hazel, "You need to pick out our room."

The two master suites were similar except one was decorated in darker colors and the one she fell in love with was more like a beach-house bedroom. The closet was big enough to be another bedroom.

"Oh, Callum. I can't believe this." She faced him. How could she have gotten so lucky?

"I take it you're willing to live here?" he asked.

"More than willing. This is wonderful."

"Good, then we'll get help bringing our things here in the morning."

"Oh, my…" She turned in another circle. "Are you sure?" Did he really want *her*?

He walked to her. "You deserve it." Sliding his hand around to her back, he pulled her to him.

"How will I ever match all this extravagance? I can never give you anything like this."

"You gave me your love, that's enough for me."

"But…"

"Shh. What is mine is yours. Never feel otherwise."

That would take some time. She'd have to get accustomed to having money. But she would never take it for granted. She appreciated him getting them a reasonably sized house. And for thinking of her profession. She would have to pinch herself every day to make sure it was real.

"I love you," she said.

"I love you, too." He kissed her.

"I want to have your baby." She kissed him.

"Let's get started right away."

She smiled against his lips. As soon as Evie was asleep, she'd like nothing more.

* * * * *

Don't miss the fourth volume in the
Coltons of Mustang Valley series,
Colton First Responder *by Linda O. Johnston,*
available now from Harlequin Romantic
Suspense!

Next month, check out Book 5—
In Colton's Custody *by Dana Nussio—*
*and Book 6—*Colton Manhunt *by Jane Godman—*
both available in March 2020!

##2079 IN COLTON'S CUSTODY
The Coltons of Mustang Valley • by Dana Nussio

After receiving a message that his daughter may have been switched at birth, Asher Colton immediately goes to the mother of the other baby to get to the bottom of things. Willow Merrill has already had her childhood ruined by the Coltons, but she reluctantly agrees to help Asher. However, neither of them expected threats to both of their lives and families!

#2080 COLTON MANHUNT
The Coltons of Mustang Valley • by Jane Godman

K-9 cop Spencer Colton blames himself for the death of his girlfriend and he'll never take another chance on love. But when dog trainer Katrina Perry is endangered while looking for her missing sister, he's forced to confront the emotional connection between them while keeping her safe.

#2081 THE RANGER'S REUNION THREAT
Rangers of Big Bend • by Lara Lacombe

Isabel Cruz has been avoiding Wyatt Spalding ever since his betrayal—after they spent one passionate night together. But someone is threatening her family and their ranch, and Wyatt is the only person who can help. Can they put their mistrust behind them long enough to stop a killer?

#2082 DEADLY TEXAS SUMMER
by Colleen Thompson

After a suspicious death on her team, environmentalist Emma Copley knows someone needs to investigate. When the authorities won't, she decides to do it herself, despite Beau Kingston's warnings. He may have a financial incentive to stop her investigation, but he certainly doesn't want her hurt. Can they trust each other long enough to find the real culprit?

She looked up at him, her expression stricken. "You don't
believe me either, do you? You don't think I can prove
that Russell was on to something real."

"I'm reserving judgment," he said, keeping his words
as steady as he could, "until I see more evidence. And
you might want to consider holding back on any more
accusations until you've recovered from this shock—and
you have that proof in hand."

"Oh, I'll find the proof. I have a good idea where, too.
All I have to do is get back to the turbines as soon as
possible and find the—"

"No way," he said sharply. "You're not going out
there. You saw the email, right? About Green Horizons'
safety review?"

She gave him a disgusted look. "Of course they want to
keep everyone away. If they're somehow involved in all

this, they'll drag out their review forever. And leave any evidence cleaned and sanitized for their own protection."

"Or they're trying to keep from being on the hook for any further accidents. Either way, I said no, Emma. I don't want you or your students taking any unnecessary chances."

"I'd never involve them. Never. After Russell, there's no way I would chance that." She shook her head, tears filling her eyes. "I was—I was the one to call Russell's parents. I insisted on it. It nearly killed me, breaking that news to them."

"Then you'll understand how I feel," Beau said, "when I tell you I'm not making that call to your folks, your boss or anyone else when you go getting yourself hurt again. Or worse."

She made a scoffing sound. "You've helped me out a couple times, sure. That doesn't make me your responsibility."

"That's where you're wrong, Dr. Copley. I take everyone who lives on, works on or sets foot on my spread as my responsibility," he said, sincerity ringing in his every word, "which is why, from this point forward, I'm barring you from Kingston property."

Don't miss
Deadly Texas Summer
by Colleen Thompson

Available March 2020 wherever
Harlequin Romantic Suspense
books and ebooks are sold.

Harlequin.com

HRSEXP0220

PRAISE FOR *PANDEMONIUM*

"*Pandemonium* is a biological battle royale: Fahy is a monster-making machine."   —Scott Sigler,
New York Times bestselling author
of the Infected trilogy

"An expertly crafted, heart-stopping tale of darkness and danger that I will not soon forget."
—Whitley Strieber,
New York Times bestselling author of
Alien Hunter

"*Pandemonium* is probably the best high-tech thriller I've read since *The Mote in God's Eye*. My heart was pounding (literally) from page one. Can't wait for his next tale."   —David Hagberg,
New York Times bestselling author of
Castro's Daughter

"If you thought *Fragment* was exciting, Warren Fahy manages to double down with *Pandemonium*!"
—Greig Beck,
author of *Beneath the Dark Ice*

PRAISE FOR *FRAGMENT*

"Fahy takes readers on a wild ride through a parallel universe where evolution has run amok—think *Jurassic Park* but scarier."   —*The Wall Street Journal*

ALSO BY WARREN FAHY

Fragment

PANDEMONIUM

WARREN FAHY

A TOM DOHERTY ASSOCIATES BOOK • NEW YORK

This is a work of fiction. All of the characters, organizations, and events portrayed in this novel are either products of the author's imagination or are used fictitiously.

PANDEMONIUM

Copyright © 2013 by Warren Fahy

Map and illustrations by Michael Limber

A Tor Book
Published by Tom Doherty Associates, LLC
175 Fifth Avenue
New York, NY 10010

www.tor-forge.com

Tor® is a registered trademark of Tom Doherty Associates, LLC.

ISBN 978-0-7653-6946-8

Tor books may be purchased for educational, business, or promotional use. For information on bulk purchases, please contact Macmillan Corporate and Premium Sales Department at 1-800-221-7945, extension 5442, or write specialmarkets@macmillan.com.

First Edition: March 2013
First Mass Market Edition: February 2014

Printed in the United States of America

0 9 8 7 6 5 4 3 2 1

ACKNOWLEDGMENTS

Thanks to Don Lovett, chair of the biology department at the University of New Jersey, for helping me design another roller coaster; Michael Limber for bringing the visuals to life; my agent, Peter McGuigan at Foundry, for greasing the rails; and Bob Gleason, for being just crazy enough to open the ride to the public.

CONTENTS